About the Author

Ali Hamdoun is an up-and-coming writer with a unique voice which he utilizes to pen down nontraditional, thought-provoking as well as engaging stories.

Welcome to Rocky Tank Town

Ali Hamdoun

Welcome to Rocky Tank Town

Olympia Publishers
London

www.olympiapublishers.com
OLYMPIA PAPERBACK

Copyright © Ali Hamdoun 2023

The right of Ali Hamdoun to be identified as author of this work has been asserted in accordance with sections 77 and 78 of the Copyright, Designs and Patents Act 1988.

All Rights Reserved

No reproduction, copy or transmission of this publication may be made without written permission.
No paragraph of this publication may be reproduced, copied or transmitted save with the written permission of the publisher, or in accordance with the provisions of the Copyright Act 1956 (as amended).

Any person who commits any unauthorized act in relation to this publication may be liable to criminal prosecution and civil claims for damage.

A CIP catalogue record for this title is available from the British Library.

ISBN: 978-1-80439-453-3

This is a work of fiction.
Names, characters, places and incidents originate from the writer's imagination. Any resemblance to actual persons, living or dead, is purely coincidental.

First Published in 2023

Olympia Publishers
Tallis House
2 Tallis Street
London
EC4Y 0AB

Dedication

À ma mère (To my mom)

PROLOGUE
SO, WHO WANTS TO SAY GRACE?

'For everything God created is good, and nothing is to be rejected if it be received with thanksgiving, because it is consecrated by the words of God and prayers.'
2 CORINTHIANS 4:15 – 16

1
ROCKY TANK TOWN, WYOMING, THANKSGIVING 1974

Close up on a Thanksgiving stuffed roasted turkey with garnish and gravy, carried on a sumptuous tray.

A stuffed turkey is brought in, carried by Marcia Misniwill, a forty-three-year-old woman wearing a navy-blue velvet dress with a white collar. She has the look of a woman with a strong character that neither bends nor breaks before adversity. Her sublime blonde hair, as fair as a field of sun-drenched wheat, is tied into a bun, which leaves one fantasizing about how attractive Marcia must be when she lets it fall freely around her face and down the nape of her neck. Her eyes alone have a bit of a mystery. They can be bewitching and sometimes petrifying to the onlooker. Oh, how enchanting they can be with their beauty so profound and yet disconcertingly mysterious, like a steely gaze piercing through a fog, hidden behind a hint of almost-psychotic seriousness. This duality of her character seems to affect her beauty, which she tries to hide behind her stern and somewhat solemn demeanor, like a religious fanatic who considers mere beauty a frivolity.

Marcia sets the tray on a large table laid out for a feast in the purest Thanksgiving tradition. At the center of the table, next to a ladle, is a large white tureen filled with pumpkin soup. There are all kinds of food like deviled eggs, sweet potato casserole, mashed potatoes and gravy, cranberry jelly, corn bread, green bean casserole, apple pie, pecan pie, pumpkin torte, a honey glazed ham, and a large pitcher of wine. Four lit candles are placed before each plate.

Sitting around the table are: Grandpa Neil Slatie, Marcia's father, a craggy-faced man in his late seventies. He is a pure neoconservative who grew up listening to stories told by his father, Christian Slatie, an adherent of American isolationism who, according to "his own" legend, once met Commodore Matthew Perry in person. Neil is a man whose mind is still deeply rooted in the past — slavery and resistance to change — and who still sees all foreigners as either niggers, monkeys or baboons, swarthy or slant, barbarians or savages and a bunch of other fanciful pernicious nicknames. His mentality perfectly matches the three principles in the manifesto that was published some twenty-four years later, in the 1996 Think Tank:

(Project for the New American Century).
1. Refusal the decline of American power because it is the first democratic world power.
2. Block the emergence of a rival power.
3. Re-evaluate the military apparatus for responding to attacks.

Sitting next to him is his wife, Stella Slatie, a seventy-five-year-old woman with gray hair who was once a radiant blonde with hair that flowed like a golden waterfall. She is a woman who was educated in the sexist tradition whereby a man decides what a woman should wear, do, say and think. Over the years, Stella's thinking has mirrored her husband's. All those years of imbibing preconceived notions gave birth to the woman sitting next to Neil. Unintentionally ignorant and somewhat submissive, yet pretending to be fulfilled, at least according to what she learned during her schooling years from 1910 to 1920. Fulfilled meant: *'Go to church every Sunday, get married very young, honor and respect your husband, have a bunch of kids who will in turn have their own children'*. Basically, be some kind of inflatable doll that can bear children.

Lastly, sitting quietly at the far end of the table, across from her grandparents, is May Sissy Misniwill — the only daughter of Marcia and Stephen Misniwill. The latter was called for duty a few days after their honeymoon and died in southern Vietnam in 1956 without knowing that his wife was pregnant with their first child. At first sight, the eighteen-year-old May Sissy seems introverted. She is fair skinned and, although she did not inherit her mother's blonde hair, she also wears hers in a bun. May Sissy was raised under the ultra-protective umbrella of her excessively religious mother, who worships her flawless idol, Jesus Christ, and never misses his service every Sunday morning. Dressed in a beautiful red velvet dress similar to her mother's, May Sissy looks uncomfortable at the sight of the giant stuffed turkey that just landed on the table in front of her, accompanied by a large cutting knife and a large fork.

Meanwhile, Grandpa Neil, drinking wine, raves on about racism and insular philosophies, sounding like the chorus of a scratched vinyl, "It is all this damn Matthew Perry's fault!"

"Blah-blah-blah." Grandma Stella interjects as she takes his glass of wine from him, "If you're trying to end up like him, you're on the right path. The doctor said no more wine. Not one glass, not even half a glass!"

But that doesn't stop him, and he continues with his 'eloquent' speech.

"He made this country what it is today! A damned market where true Americans can't take a quiet walk without running into niggers or slants…"

Marcia cuts him off adamantly, "Please, Father, not now." She gives him a cold look, as she puts the turkey tray on the table.

May Sissy keeps staring at the roasted stuffed turkey laid before her. She looks increasingly uncomfortable; her face goes pale as her mother, Marcia, about to carve the turkey, asks in a solemn voice, "So, who wants to say grace? May Sissy?"

She gives her daughter an authoritative look that clearly says, '*This is not a request. It is an order young girl.*'

There is a moment of silence during which May Sissy hesitates, avoiding her mother's eyes. She stares at her thin pale hands. Then she raises her eyes and glances peculiarly at the stuffed turkey, like someone starting to get overwhelmed by sudden nausea at the sight of an unbearable spectacle. While her grandparents are waiting for her to respond, Marcia is growing impatient and a nervous grin appears on her face as the seconds tick by. Holding the large cutting knife and the fork in each hand, Marcia stares expectantly at her daughter, her eyes as cold as that of an angel of death with the power to give or take life. This moment certainly feels like a heavy hammer hovering threateningly above the fragile-looking May Sissy, who finally decides to stand up and say grace in an unsteady voice, like a young nervous actress performing on stage for the very first time:

"For everything God created is good, and nothing is to be rejected if it is received with thanksgiving, because it is consecrated by the word of God and prayer. For all things are for your sake, so that the grace which is spreading to more and more people may cause the giving of thanks to abound to the glory of God. Give thanks to the Lord, for he is good; his love endures forever. Amen."

Marcia gives May Sissy a stern but yet affectionate look that says: *'See, it wasn't that hard'* as she, Grandpa Neil and Grandma Stella say in unison, "Amen."

Marcia is about to cut the turkey when May Sissy interrupts her, visibly unable to contain her aversion for what her mother is about to do. May Sissy rises up again, rubs her arm nervously, and declares in a feverish voice — as if she was about to announce, *'I'm pregnant'* — under the puzzled look of her grandparents and the suspicious stare of her mother, apparently fearing the worst, "I-I-I... I've decided to become a vegetarian."

Marcia now has a petrified gaze; it is as if her daughter has voiced out the ultimate blasphemy.

May Sissy's frail reflection appears in the blade of the knife Marcia still holds in her hand...

CHAPTER ONE
A FOX, A PIT BULL TERRIER, AN EXOTIC BIRD & A BROWN BEAR

1
Welcome to Rocky Tank Town

NOVEMBER 21, 2012
The American flag and the flag of Wyoming flap high at the entrance of Rocky Tank Town, a small town located in Niobrara County. This community seems unaffected by the passing of time or rather time seems to have stopped moving for this town long ago. The poor town has always been ignored by its neighboring counties, including its own county, Niobrara, as if it was a plagued place or a town under perpetual quarantine. Rocky Tank Town is also erroneously called 'The Basin'. Sometimes, the most imaginative people even call it 'Toilet Pan'. Indeed, it seems that Rocky Tank Town was established in the center of an enormous granitic crater surrounded by a huge forest and a mountain hidden behind a white haze. This scenery could inspire any young horror writer desperately seeking inspiration.

The entrance to the town begins right where the great forest called The Red Bear ends. A huge pine forest surrounding Rocky Tank Town. This vast landscape of trees stretching as far as the eye can see, towering over Rocky Tank Town is a chilling sight that gives the uneasy feeling of being watched or spied on at all times by these immutable, majestic monolith-like giant pines standing upright like stoic guards attempting to preserve a town deliberately forgotten by modern society. It is the last bastion standing up to a society that is too often eager for an opportunity to grow richer while others see a naive, fragile and increasingly precarious wilderness.

On the other side, across from the forest, a mountain towers high above the landscape. It is no Mount Everest, but it blocks the view of a considerable part of the north east. Apart from the immense pine forest, this mountain feels like the starting point of life, the first witness of life and time, the past, the present and even the future — like a gigantic shaman — like entity, holding the key to our truth.

An imposing wrought iron sign is suspended on a pole at the entrance of Rocky Tank Town, with these words carved in golden letters:

'WELCOME TO ROCKY TANK TOWN'

The main street is called Rusty Street, a coal-black cobbled street that glistens in the rain. It ends at a junction a little further down. The houses on Rusty Street have quite antiquated and obsolete architecture. The only drugstore in Rocky Tank Town is squeezed between two houses. No bigger than a mini-mart, this drugstore has a rather inviting facade, compared to the rest of the dark houses and silent surroundings. The light and icy rain falling over the small town seems to carry some kind of a protective aura. It is as though the sky is crying tears of compassion and love over Rocky Tank Town, forming a wet dome which gives the small town a somewhat supernatural appearance imbued with a certain fascinating Gothicism.

Rocky Tank Town is an extremely conservative community of Republican traditionalists who boast of its racist past, advocating slavery. The first and only Afro-American family in Rocky Tank Town moved there in December 1967. Most of the townspeople are descendants of English families. Although racism has decreased over the years, the conservative mentality in the community remains unchanged.

A taxi pulls up at the entrance of Rocky Tank Town. A man named Martial Sillons, carrying a black travel bag climbs out from the back seat. He pays the taxi driver and turns around to face the entrance of this small town where he moved to with his mother in 1967 when he was fourteen years old. Today, he is fifty-nine years old. He is wearing a gray wool winter coat, and, apart from his graying short hair and beard, the clean features of his face make him look ten years younger than he really is.

Martial then says to himself with a disillusioned voice, "Well, well. Good old 'Toilet Pan'!" He giggles nervously, then adds, "Well, I can see why. This town does look like it was formed in a crater shaped like some gigantic shitter."

Holding his big black travel bag at arm's length, Martial looks up at the sign that says, 'WELCOME TO ROCKY TANK TOWN'. Cocking his head, he stares lengthily at the sign with bitterness. Martial has no good childhood memories in Rocky Tank Town except maybe for one sweet memory called May Sissy. She was his very first love, if it can be called love. Their story could have ended in almost the same tragic manner as that of Romeo and Juliet if Martial had not left the town in 1970 in order to help his old uncle run a chainsaw shop somewhere in Oregon, leaving his mother alone in this 'shithole'. After his uncle died, Martial became a sergeant in the Portland police department, putting aside his dream of ever becoming a veterinarian or an animal rights advocate, because as he often said, *'Some dream of a simple and peaceful life, but they become rich bastards full of themselves. Others dream of becoming rich bastards full of themselves, but they end up having a simple and peaceful life.'*

Staring at the entrance sign, Martial says to himself in a low disillusioned voice, "Yeah, not so sure about this."

Finally, Martial crosses the entrance and walks down Rusty Street, empty and silent, just like a ghost town devoid of life.

He walks inside the town, moving down Rusty Street, echo-like ghostly remnant aimlessly wandering about, drenched in the rain that falls from the darkened sky.

2

Martial is now walking on Grand Street, which branches off Rusty Street and leads to the center of Rocky Tank Town where one can find the library, the school, the church, a small bookstore (selling mainly old items) and other small shops. Martial walks down Grand Street, a paved alley with splendid electric lamps set twenty-four feet apart, giving the alley a charming Londoner look. There is a row of beautiful houses along either side of the street, each house facing another.

As he walks down the street holding his travel bag, Martial looks wryly at the houses around him. He stops at a house and heads for the beautiful azure blue front door with a wind chime.

He stands at the door and he raises a fist to knock, but changes his mind and stays a few seconds in the doorway, undecided…

Finally, he decides to knock on the door. As he waits for a response, he hears a strange noise that sounds like a biscuit being crushed. He looks down and realizes that he has just stepped on some cookies right in front of the door. Even more surprising, than finding cookies outside his mother's house, is a little fox standing on its four legs just beside him. The fox seems to look at Martial skeptically (if a fox can be skeptical). Martial looks at the fox in surprise and says in a gentle voice, "Hey, what are you doing here, little guy? Are you lost?"

Looking at the biscuits he unintentionally crushed, Martial understands that the cookies were left there for the fox. Martial puts his bag down and starts to pick up some crumbs off the ground. Scared by the stranger, the fox begins to growl, baring its teeth. In a nonthreatening tone, Martial says to the fox, "It's okay, buddy." He holds out the crumbs to the fox and says, "Here."

Suspicious at first, the fox cautiously approaches Martial's hand. He smells the cookie crumbs and finally starts eating them. Martial says, "There you go. Sorry, buddy, but if you trust that sign at the entrance, you won't see the end of winter."

Suddenly, the front door opens, and Mindy Sillons, Martial's mother is standing in the doorway. She is about to turn seventy-four. Mindy Sillons says to Martial, "Ah! I see you met my little friend."

Martial says, "Hi, Mom."

Oddly enough, around his mother, Martial doesn't look like a robust fifty-nine-year-old man at all, but like a small boy with gentle eyes. He steps forward and hugs his mother. His mother looks so happy to have her only son visit her.

She hugs him, saying, "Oh, it's been such a long time!"

"Indeed," Martial replies.

"Well, come on in!" says Mindy. "Come on in! You're not going to stay in the doorway like a scarecrow now, are you?"

Martial picks up his black travel bag that he had set on the floor next to him and walks into his mother's house.

The front door shuts behind them.

3

Martial is sitting at the coffee table, a rather mundane wooden table covered with a tablecloth made of thin white lace, which is much less common than the table it covers. Embroidered in the middle of the tablecloth is a beautiful fountain with birds drinking from both sides. Two beautiful turquoise birds below a banner with dark red contours and a sublime inscription *SACRA ALITE DOMINI* (the sacred birds of the Lord). At each end of the embroidered tablecloth is a small fountain with similar birds. Martial contemplates the drawing in a distracted manner. Then his gaze leaves the tablecloth and wanders off into the lounge with fascination. Martial hasn't set foot in this room in a very long time. His eyes and the expression on his face is that of someone trying to figure if everything is still where it was when he left. He realizes with amusement that some of the items have been replaced over the years. But the biggest change in the living room is that there is now a TV placed on a beautiful mahogany cabinet facing a massive green leather sofa perfectly maintained despite its age of forty-seven years. Fortunately, only Mindy has sat on it most of the time. As he continues contemplating the sofa, an impish grin creeps onto Martial's face, causing him to make the following

reflection, *This dear old couch must surely be the only one to appreciate the racist mentality of Rocky Tank Town.* His internal voice always has this caustic tone with just a hint of melancholy. Between the couch and the TV is an old low wooden table, massive and covered with a white cloth on which is embroidered a drawing of a black man wearing a navy-blue jumpsuit picking the earth under the sun. Next to it is a drawing of the same man, this time using a pick to unearth gold as yellow as maize. Embroidered in the center is a slogan:
'SWEAT IS PROOF OF HARD WORK'.

Martial seems lost in thought while Mindy returns from the kitchen with two cups of hot coffee and a tray with a small plate of corn bread. Humorously, she says, "So, you finally decided to visit your old mother."

For a seventy-three-year-old woman, Mindy is a cultivated modern woman, full of energy who loves to be in touch with each new generation. She has always had a strong curiosity which, for a woman, particularly a black woman at that time, was considered as slyness in a macho community headed by men who feared that one day knowledge and wisdom would fall into the hands of women.

With an affectionate smile, Martial says to his mother, "Yeah. But she's not that old."

Sitting down, Mindy says, "Oh, please! You know how I'm allergic to smooth talk!"

"And compliments too, I see," he says teasing her with a smile. "Maybe you're getting a little too old and sour for this after all."

Martial and his mother have always been close, and they never miss an opportunity to tease each other. And as her face lights up with pride, Mindy says to Martial, "Ah, look at you!

Obama himself is in my house!"

To which Martial says slightly amused, "Yeah, well your Obama has gained a bit of weight then."

Mindy turns to Martial and says, "You can take off your coat, you know. Life in the city has made you all suspicious, or what?

"You can rest assured, there's no thief in this house."

Martial then realizes that he's still wearing his coat and says, "Oh, yeah."

His mother then asks, "How is Amanda?"

Martial tries to evade the subject and briefly says, "Don't know."

Martial's face becomes sadder, paler; his mind wanders off, far from his mother's house. Mindy sees it immediately and hastens to tell him while putting her hand on his in a tender and affectionate gesture, "Well, I'm glad you're here to celebrate Thanksgiving with me. I'm so happy to see you. That's all that matters."

"Me too, Mom." He strokes his mother's hand affectionately and one more time, he says, "Me too."

Ever since his mother spoke the name 'Amanda', Martial has been looking deeply disturbed. His gaze shifts constantly as if his mind struggles to confine some painful memory within the bowels of the past.

"I'm glad you're here. You're going to help me prepare our Thanksgiving meal," Mindy says.

Martial seems a bit surprised and says, "Prepare the Thanksgiving meal? Um, you know that has never really been my thing." On a self-deprecating note, he adds, "I'm more likely to offend the big guy up there. Do you really want me to go to hell?"

"God is merciful and if he forgave those who crucified his son, I'm pretty sure he will forgive some awkwardness," responds Mindy in a complicit tone.

"Yeah, well I think he won't be so merciful once I help you prepare the Thanksgiving meal."

"Well, you may be right after all. Maybe I should handle that meal on my own."

"Now, that makes a lot more sense!"

With a teasing smile, Mindy says, "You do know that sloth is a sin, even when it's disguised as a so-called ineptitude." Martial looks at his mother in a way that seems to say, *'Okay, you got me!'* Martial's personality has changed over time. He now seems much quieter, almost tortured. He gives furtive glances, his eyes sweeping through the lounge or looking at his hands or shoes but never directly at his mother.

No longer able to endure this monastic silence, hardly disturbed by the sound of a spoon Martial absent-mindedly holds, Mindy asks, "How long do you plan to stay?"

"Just a few days."

"Why don't you go take a stroll around the neighborhood."

"Yeah, I'll do that."

His mind wanders off. He gets up, tapping gently on the table with the flat of his hand. He sips his coffee and says sarcastically, "Let's go see if this charming neighborhood is the same as back then."

With his back straight, wearing his gray woolen winter coat and holding his cup in one hand while staring gravely through the window, lost in thought, Martial looks like President Obama thinking about the speech he's about to make before the senate. Except that it is doubtful any president ever walked into the senate chamber holding a cup of coffee.

Martial takes another sip of his coffee, puts the cup down and in a sarcastic and bitter voice, he says, "Mellow and welcoming."

He grabs his bag, but his mother gets up quickly and says, "Oh, leave it. Come on! I'm not that old yet, you know! I can still handle my little boy's stuff."

She looks at him and realizes that he is a good head taller than she is. "Well, perhaps not so little any more."

Martial caresses his mother's cheek affectionately and says, "And I am not yet old enough to stop being your little boy."

4
1859

Martial stands in his childhood bedroom, in front of his bed, mentally assessing the room. The bedroom is not the same any more. It used to be decorated from the ceiling to the floor. The ceiling was covered with a gigantic poster of the Shadows above the bed. Bed in which Martial had so many nightmares, and a lot of wonderful dreams too. Now of course, there were also the little private matters that we'd rather forget once we reach adulthood. Stuff like the first attempts at jerking off while fantasizing about different actresses or a singer like Aretha Franklin, although Martial never dared masturbate while thinking about her. Probably because, he had too much respect for the lady she was to him. Not that those other women did not deserve the same respect! Or maybe she reminded him too much of his own mother. That's rather unsettling in this kind of situation!

The room once littered with all kinds of things; its four walls entirely covered with posters of Chuck Berry and the Shadows, now looks ordinary and trite, with simple decoration. All the posters are gone and there's nothing left of what it was like to be a youth in the '60s. Beside the bed is a cherrywood dresser and nothing else. His poor room is totally different from what it used to be. Even his beloved giant poster of The Shadows — the very same picture on the cover photo of *The Shadows by Themselves*, snapped by Royston Ellis in 1961 — that he had pinned to the ceiling is no longer there.

Martial puts his black travel bag on the bed. He digs into the inside pocket of his coat and takes out his wallet, made of a supple deep mahogany leather wallet on which is embroidered the number 1859. Martial stares at the number embroidered on the wallet. Now that he thinks about it, he hasn't the foggiest idea about this number. *Was the wallet made in the year 1859?*

Perhaps the wallet factory was created in that year? If that was the case, there would be a brand tag on it... perhaps the brand is 1859...?

5
W. D. G

JULY 1997, PORTLAND
Martial is in his son's room, Lawrence Tyrese, inside their single-floor house. He reads through a diary on Lawrence Tyrese's desk, which was open to a page that Martial reads with interest. Martial is wearing a simple short-sleeved khaki t-shirt and black pants.

As Martial reads through the page, his demeanor becomes

more intense. An involuntary half-incredulous frown plays timidly on Martial's face. He grabs the diary and continues reading it, leaning against the foot of the bed in a half-seated position.

The size of the room is about 5m by 7m — the entrance wall and the wall parallel to it. There are two windows on the wall, parallel to the entrance wall, one on the right and one on the left, separated by about 2.5m of wall space. Each window is 110cm by 135cm, located 75cm from the floor. Off white — somewhat yellowish — Venetian blinds cover the two windows. The blind on the right, which is above Lawrence's desk, is completely closed while the one located 2.5m further on the left is slightly open, letting in a faint, dusty beam of light. The flooring has lost its past luster due to long use. Its color is grayish in some areas, creating a strange and disconcerting illusion of magnetizing the dusty light beam which is of a similar color.

Drops trickle down Martial's neck, which may be blamed on the stifling heat in the house but are really the last witnesses of a refreshing shower that Martial just had.

The semi-darkness in the room gives it a strange lugubrious aura. The room is a mess, with a slightly chaotic decoration. A pair of neglected jeans with a belt dangle pitiably from the back rest of the chair that is tilted slightly toward the left side of the desk. The desk is a Teck double frame desk with the following dimensions: H77 x B153 x W92. It has six drawers that are incorporated into the massive legs of the furniture, three drawers per leg. The desk lies against the wall on the right, perpendicular to the entrance wall. The desk is about 60cm from the window which lies to the left. Meanwhile, a bit further to the right of the desk is a fairly old bookshelf with five plain levels made of rustic wood, just like the rest of the bookshelf. The bookshelf is 190cm in height, 150cm in breadth and 35cm in depth.

A wardrobe made of brown wood lies against the entrance wall. The door of the wardrobe has a mirror. On the same wall, between the entrance door and the wardrobe, is a Mara-colored wooden dresser. The dresser is 120cm in breadth, 46cm in depth and 77cm in height. On the dresser, there is a stuffed Uromastyx which is missing a fourth of its right upper leg. The lizard measures about 50cm, which is rather small for an adult lizard. A little further, there is a TV/VCR Combo set as well as VHS tapes such as *Jurassic Park*, *Bill & Ted's Excellent Adventure*, *Bill & Ted's Bogus Journey*, *Clerks*, John Carpenter's *They Live*, 1989's *Warlock*, *The Death of the Incredible Hulk*, *Hercules in New York* and 1986 Sondra Locke's *Ratboy*. Higher up, on the fifth level of the bookshelf, there is an imposing action figure of Hot Rodimus Prime — measuring about 35cm — which Lawrence got for the Christmas of 1986. Just above the toy is the poster of *The Transformers: The Movie* — measuring 28cm x 43cm — pinned to the wall. It was the very first movie that Lawrence saw with his father at the cinema, and the sense of wonder that he felt then was one of those rare unforgettable experiences that left a mark on the inexperienced and innocent mind of Lawrence, who was five and a half years old at that time, still uninitiated to any of the inherent lassitude and deception of any existence on the Earth. While the movie was being shown, Lawrence, captivated by the scene playing out, made this mental note *Dad is the best dad ever!* while devouring his popcorn. He was overcome with a sense of pride and another feeling that he was not yet familiar with: Gratitude. These unfathomable moments of utter euphoria which seem to distort time. Making every single moment from childhood memorable. Shielded inside this nebulous protective dome. It is a bit sad to realize that childhood is more or less like lightning in a bottle, stored in the depths of this empyrean cocoon of memory, destined to eventually, inevitably become this dusty, fading abstract, chimerical mirage.

On the second shelf from the top, are ten wonderfully preserved Starting Lineup Kemer action figures, 1992 USA MLB, NFL, NHL, NBA Basketball Team, proudly displayed.

The walls are generously covered with numerous posters. The poster of the *White Men Can't Jump* is pinned just above the desk. Between the bookshelf and the door is the black-and-white poster of Muhammad Ali taunting Sonny Liston, showing Muhammad Ali standing over Sonny Liston and taunting him to get up during their title fight at the Central Maine Youth Center in Lewiston, Maine. Against the bedroom door is a black-and-white poster of LL Cool J carrying a boom box on his right shoulder while posing for a studio portrait in 1985, New York. He is wearing a Kangol Bermuda casual hat, earrings, several necklaces, and a leather jacket. Above the Uromastyx, there is a color poster of LL Cool J with E Love and B-Rock, Manhattan, New York, 1987. Between the wardrobe and the bed is a black-and-white 1996 poster of Subcomandante Marcos smoking a pipe, on horseback in Chiapas, Mexico. Lastly, just above the bed, there is a poster of Nas' *Illmatic*.

Lawrence's room is a perfect illustration of what the room of children — including adolescents — should be; a comforting sanctuary, unstained by the bitterness, cynicism, toxicity of the outside world.

At this moment, Lawrence enters into his room, finding his father engrossed in his diary, in the same half-seated position against the bed, facing his son's desk on top of which lay Lawrence's wallet, made of beautiful supple deep mahogany leather, on which is embroidered 1859. Meanwhile, at the foot of the bed is Lawrence's old and precious 1985 waste bin, bearing the image of his favorite character, Marvin the Martian.

Lawrence Tyrese is a slim young man with short hair, dressed in black sweatpants and a short-sleeved shirt just like his father's.

"Dad?" he exclaims warily.

Martial looks up, fixes his half-perplexed half-questioning gaze on Lawrence and starts reading aloud from his son's notebook:

"Museum of disposable ethnicities Obsolete tools out of line."

"Get a decade-long W.D.G treatment Doggystyle becoming a fuckin lifestyle?"

Martial pauses, gives a disapproving look and then continues, "And red is now in black and white upon the pavement While everyone else is suddenly color blind."

"It's part of a short freestyle rap/poem that I wrote. It is harsh and all but I kinda like it that way." Lawrence calmly explains in a prudent but detached tone.

"What does it mean?" Martial asks in a lenient tone that is, however, not bereft of a hint of disapproval. His face wore a thoughtful expression which can sometimes be mistaken for apathy or indifference.

Lawrence immediately starts to explain in a didactic tone with a nearly imperceptible hint of enthusiasm, "Well, obsolete slaves or blacks out of line get a decade-long W. D. G treatment…"

"What's a W. D. G treatment?" asks Martial in this same lenient tone, attentive but a bit curious.

Lawrence immediately answers this question in the same passionate didactic tone, "W, wars. D, drugs. G, guns. W. D. G treatment," Lawrence pauses briefly. He observes his father with a quick glance, as if to confirm that they are on the same page, and then continues, "Bend over, or kowtow. You know, getting used to being treated like trash.

"And, as long as it's black folks, red blood on the pavement is black and white. It doesn't matter."

Martial, pensive, appears to be dubious, somewhat skeptical. After a brief moment of reflection, Martial speaks up once more in the same indulgent and thoughtful tone, "You know, your message could still be that impactful without the use of vulgar language. Listen, I get that you want to be part of something bigger than yourself. I get it. Trust me." Martial then pauses for a brief moment. He appears to be putting his thoughts together, and then continues his tacit encouragement, "Using abusive language is not automatically a proof of bravery. In writing, it can be seen as a lack of imagination. You can't win an argument with insults. Be poetic and original. If you are going to take this Rapping thing seriously, then start by respecting words. Poor word choices can be detrimental to your message, but the right words can cause a whole lot of damage… You could use the word coercion, for example. It would help to convey your message."

"So, I take it that you're not a big fan of N. W. A, huh?" retorts Lawrence in a light-hearted, playful tone.

"And where the hell did you get to listen to N. W. A?"

Martial asks in a fit of false anger. Lawrence, caught by surprise, hardly has time to answer his father's question.

"Ah! I can't keep up with this generation," Martial says in a feigned resigned tone, before almost immediately following it with, "By the way, since when do you know about doggystyle?" in a slightly shocked tone.

"Well… I-I…" Lawrence stutters. It is one of those moments when you wish you could be anywhere else but here. You wish you could temporarily pull the plug, temporarily disconnect from your body and retire to the safety of the personal and impenetrable bubble that is our mind. This, is the perfect illustration of what is going on in Lawrence's mind right now: Krang inside his humanoid robot.

However, Lawrence is woken up from his brief, self-imposed escape-like reverie.

"Are you still… I mean, have you already done it?" Martial asks prudishly in a reproaching tone.

"Dad! No. You watched *Boyz n the Hood* way too many times!" Lawrence protests. "Oh, because you've watched *Boyz n the Hood*, too!" Martial exclaims.

"You know. I have my ways." Lawrence replies in a prudent tone as his face wears a respectful, mischievous but not irreverent expression. Lawrence's ways can be found in one of his VHSs, in this case *Back to the Future III*.

"Oh, you have your ways, huh! Well, if you don't want your mother's foot finding its way up your butt, you better be smarter about it. You can be sure that your mother will not be so lenient," Martial retorts, taking a quick glance at the poster of LL Cool J and giving Lawrence a knowing look. "Because you know your mamma will most definitely knock you out."

Lawrence and his father give each other a knowing look

and both of them have a smile on their faces. After this short pause, Martial adds in a slightly more serious tone that still has a hint of slight leniency, "And the only F word that should come out of your mouth better be the right one. Now clean up your room. Now you can use the F word."

Reluctantly, Lawrence says, "Fine."

It is true that the room is somewhat messy and dusty. The bed is not made and Lawrence's CD player with its speakers are on it. The CD in the Walkman is Rage Against The Machine's Evil Empire. Martial is about to leave his son's room when Lawrence says in a strangely mature tone while blankly staring into the abyss, "You know, Dad, we can't spend our lives wearing blinders."

"Yeah… I get that. I respect and admire your way of expressing yourself, but I also know too well how much the truth can be a white elephant in this world we're living in," Martial calmly replies, with bitter melancholy on his face.

Then there is a moment of silence, during which Martial and Lawrence stare into their own personal darkness.

"Do you sometimes wonder what Nyssa would've been like?" asks Lawrence. "I wonder what kind of big brother I would've been to her… if I had the chance to…"

"You… You would've been as… Your mother and I would've been as proud of you being a big brother as we are of you being our son."

Martial wants to say more but he knows better than to follow this corrupting, poisonous white rabbit into his hole… into this limbo of painful memories. One minute you are the happiest father in the whole world, holding your premature newborn infant… and three months later…

"Is it normal to miss non-existing memories?" Lawrence

asks, still staring into the void. "I miss us, me and her arguing over stupid things…"

Once more, a silence settles in, a sepulchral silence which imparts an almost graveyard-like aura to the room. Martial glances over the room distractedly and looks at his son briefly, affliction written all over his face, the look of a father who is temporarily emotionally helpless, unable to comfort his son. Unable to comfort himself.

Finally, after a thirty seconds-long eternity, Martial leaves his son's bedroom.

6

Martial opens his wallet to reveal a photograph. It shows Martial with his wife, Amanda — Puerto Rican African-American from her mother's side and Jamaican African-American from her father's side — and their only son, sixteen-year-old Lawrence Tyrese Sillons. The picture was taken in 1997. Amanda wore a gorgeous green Veronese Poncho pullover with rounded bottom and vertical stripes which joined toward the bottom to form a V. Four stripes ran from the right shoulder; grayish green, bright blue azure, lapis lazuli blue, white, and four similar stripes ran from the left shoulder: Venetian yellow (or sometimes simply called Venetian), fawn, cobalt yellow and new gamboge.

As Martial looks at the picture with deep sadness, a tear wells up in the corner of his eye, slowly rolling down his cheek. A tear, quickly followed by several others, falls on the plastic sleeve enclosing the photos. Martial attempts to pull himself together, wiping his eyes but unable to hold back this deep grief. He sits on the edge of the bed and surrenders to the expression of his sorrow. All his grief pours out of him like a torrential cascade fleeing this hermetic bruised shell. The tears roll off the plastic sleeve, dropping onto the floor. He weeps loudly, holding his head in his hands. Finally, Martial manages to pull himself together. He wipes his tears; he is in pain and his face looks as though shards of glass were being pulled from it. His mental anguish feels worse than physical pain. The worst kind of affliction is often psychological. Martial slides his fingers behind the two photos and takes out four small black-and-white photos that were taken on September 16, 1968 in a photo booth at the entrance of the mini-market in Rocky Tank Town center. They are about the size of passport photos, about an inch and a half wide and an inch and three quarters high, in a vertical strip, showing fifteen-year-old Martial and twelve and a half-year-old May Sissy. Both goofy faced in the four pictures, they look so carefree and full of childhood innocence.

7

Martial strolls down Grand Street, his hands in his pockets, looking curiously at the surrounding houses. Everything feels so new to him. Thin raindrops fall from the cloudy sky. Were it not for the orange hues of dusk in the sky, it would have been almost impossible to say whether the time was seven a.m. or seven p.m. The architecture on the street appears to intrigue Martial. His eyes linger on each house, lamppost and other new features that were added after he left Rocky Tank Town. The street isn't the same any more, which is quite frankly a good thing. Honestly, Grand Street once looked more like the Red-Light District of London back in the days of Jack the

Ripper. Martial moves toward the end of the street and heads for the center of Rocky Tank Town, where three of the four streets of Rocky Tank Town converge. It would seem that the town was designed by someone with a keen interest in labyrinths. Rusty Street starts at the entrance of Rocky Tank Town and ends with Grand Street branching to the right, and on the left R. A. Minnesota Avenue, named after the founder of Rocky Tank Town — Richard Arthur Minnesota. Both Grand Street and R. A. Minnesota Avenue eventually reach the other side to pour into the center of Rocky Tank Town. A third small street called Raven's Feather winds on the extreme left after Grand Street.

8

Dusk begins to cover the sky, a beautiful gradient going from pale yellow orange to deep orange. Martial stands at the end of Grand Street just outside the center of Rocky Tank Town.

A rather grand library, an old building that seems to be built on unshakable foundations, stands between Raven's Feather and R. A. Minnesota Avenue. Next to the library is the school, rather large for such a small town. The building serves as the primary, middle and high school. Martial realizes that this place, with its wrought iron gate, is by far the most beautiful building to look at. Then there is the mini-market. Seeing it, Martial wonders if the photo booth in which he and May Sissy took the pictures still exists. Martial can't deny that time has somehow played in favor of this place. The ground is now paved. There are no holes that may cause people to stumble. The mini-market looks bigger than it used to be and, compared to 1967, its facade seems more impressive today.

There is a bookstore right after the mini-market:

ROSE & PAKQUARD BOOKSTORE

Then next to the bookstore is the bakery and butchery. Between R. A. Minnesota Avenue and Grand Street stands the Church, so tall that its shadow covers the middle of the town center. Towering over the surrounding buildings which look ridiculously small in comparison. Standing there, ominously immutable, with an imposing monolithic stature reminiscent of the architecture of a Gothic cathedral built from what looks like some sort of black granite. The building looks nothing like a simple neighborhood church. Standing tall like a guardian, striking the perfect balance between order and morality (at least religious), like a reminder for the people of Rocky Tank Town, insinuating into their thoughts every time they pass by, *'I see you. I'm watching you. Do not forget; your every move, your every action, nothing escapes me.*

'P.S: Watch out, because once up there, there might be Hell to pay!'

Next to the church, stands the only bar in the Town. These two sanctuaries stand so close to each other, and yet could not be farther apart. Either the goody two-shoes were completely inebriated with wine during the final decision regarding the layout of the church, or the bottle lovers covered their rears by sticking their buttocks to those of God. One would almost expect to see Moe Szyslak and Reverend Lovejoy come out simultaneously from their respective shrines.

Martial turns his attention to the church and then down Raven's Feather. Everything related to the evil twin of Existence is fully represented in Raven's Feather (Cemetery,

Funeral Service). Being on a slight slope, Raven's Feather ends with a second entrance opposite the main entrance of Rocky Tank Town, which is on Rusty Street. This secondary entrance serves more as an exit, for people mostly leave town through it. Built as a bow buttress forming just behind the center of the town, Raven's Feather shelters some houses, and is quite honestly the most pleasant street: peaceful, inviting us for a somnambular deambulation, guided by the sweet warmth of the lampposts along the street.

Martial's eyes then stop on a detail he had not noticed up until now. A detail that was not present when he left the town in '70. And, talk about a detail! A ten and a half feet long 'detail' set in the center of a rotary; a massive stuffed brown bear dominating the center of the town. Its mouth wide open, its paws raised up, and a nasty menacing look.

Suddenly, the school bell rings sharply. Children and teenagers come out running in a boisterous hurly-burly of blissfulness, happy to finally blow off some steam without getting in trouble. Some of the teenagers leave quietly alone; others leave in groups. Martial realizes that some things do not change and probably never will. As indeed, school exits seem the ideal place to observe the embodiment of the term 'cliché'. There are all kinds of individuals, each belonging to a universe of their own. Martial observes the pupils leaving school. There are the Goths, who are more or less withdrawn. There are also those that seem to be leaving a convent rather than a school. There are others who seem to follow no trend in particular.

A bit surprised, Martial looks at his watch. *Isn't it a bit late for school to end just now? Surely these kids must have stayed behind to study after class.* As he used to back in his days. But, to his surprise, it is only 4:45 p.m.!

Martial then closes his eyes, as if to remember, to briefly reconnect with the past. And while the last students come out, Martial lets his mind wander through distant memories…

9

Memories, memories…
Unfortunately, I cannot remember this distant time. Memories, memories…
For I keep remembering only some fragments. Would it be a crime?

Ring, Ring, Ring! Ring, Ring, Ring! Don't you hear?
It's the sound of your freedom.
Now you are free to run, run, run, run!
What are you waiting for?
Don't you hear?
Now it's time to forget all you've learned!

10

SEPTEMBER 16, 1968
Fifteen-year-old Martial stands at the school entrance, as all around him, students are running, heckling, and shouting. Some of them come out silently, clutching their books and notebooks like Holy Bibles. Standing motionless and staring ahead blankly, for this godforsaken hole in which Martial had landed in spite of himself was indeed a godforsaken hole, an interstellar void that would make for the most boring adventure of the USS Enterprise. He looks at this charming emptiness in a distant way. In these transcendental, cathartic moments, Martial likes to let his mind wander off far away to

some imaginary land, utopic realm, in fact anywhere but here... like right now. Martial is repeating mechanically while closing his eyes as if escaping a terrible nightmare, "Anywhere but here... Anywhere but here..."

Lost in this cathartic escape, Martial doesn't realize the presence of a trio of vindictive students.

Dickhead 1 rudely says to an apathetic Martial, "Move out of the way pinhead!"

While Dickhead 2 knocks Martial out of the way with his elbow and says mockingly, "Hey! The sidewalk doesn't belong to you, you know!"

But it seems — correction: It's undeniable — that Dickhead 3 is the one with the richest vocabulary,

"Sure thing, dude!"

The students laugh out loud as they walk away. Martial closes his eyes slowly, still repeating mechanically, "Anywhere but here... Anywhere but here... Anywhere but here... Anywhere but here..." while standing at the epicenter of this pleasant, comforting emptiness, listening to his own voice echo throughout this personal immensity.

However, his spiritual journey is now interrupted by a voice that sounds distant and unreal in his ears, like the sweet and bewitching voice of a mermaid, "What are you doing? What are you waiting for? Didn't you hear?"

The voice is indistinct, drowned by an invisible mist, just like when someone is shouting out in the middle of a snowstorm. Martial realizes that the distant voice is real. He opens his eyes again and discovers May Sissy Misniwill standing right in front of him. She is only twelve and a half years old though she appears to be nearly fourteen. Her beautiful hair is in one long braid and sways from side to side like a mesmeric pendulum. May Sissy is like a sublime exotic bird that hates being locked in the cage. Like a ticking bomb that's ready to explode upon the strike of the hour.

Immersed in his thoughts, Martial almost forgot May Sissy, the only person who sees him not as a nigger but as a real friend, her best friend. May Sissy looks at Martial with her insistent but yet mesmerizing and disconcerting look. She wears a long thick woolen winter coat with three color bands, arranged in a gradient from darkest to lightest, from brown to beige and pinkish beige near the cuff. Her beautiful long braid falls on her hood with the same gradient behind it, giving her the appearance of an Inuit. Her coat is closed by four clasps attached around four black buttons (each with two small holes in the middle). She holds some schoolbooks in her arms.

"What are you doing? What are you waiting for? Don't you hear? You plan to stay there until they reopen school tomorrow morning or what? Come on, Martial!" She then adds with gusto, "Now it's time to forget all you've learned and enjoy life!"

"Isn't your mother going to scold you if you get home late?" Martial says.

May Sissy replies, "No, she's in Cheyenne for the weekend. She went to visit my old aunt. She's a pain in the ass."

"Cheyenne, huh?" "Yeah."

"Didn't know you had an aunt in Cheyenne."

"Yeah. Everyone has at least one aunt or uncle. Me, it's my aunt Anna, my mother's older sister. She lives in some hellhole in Cheyenne."

"I heard Cheyenne was a nice place."

To which May Sissy retorts, "Yeah, maybe for those who

don't go there to visit their old aunt who's dying of pneumonia."

Martial slowly nods in acknowledgment.

It's extremely cold for September. Martial is grateful that his mother advised him to take his thick winter hat with him *'just in case'*. Martial is also wearing a brown leather bag strapped over his shoulders. It has some wear in the right places, giving it a weathered look, which gives him a certain sense of style. Unlike May Sissy, he carries no books in his hands.

Martial blows in his hands to warm himself and says, "It's freezing out here! Why don't we find someplace warm to sit? I can't feel my fingers any more."

May Sissy immediately suggests, "How about the mini-market?" Martial, not very enthusiastic, asks, "The mini-market?"

May Sissy seems excited, unlike Martial. She jumps up and down to get warm and replies, "Yeah! They've got a photo booth there!"

"A photo booth?" says Martial inquisitively.

"Yeah, you know… Like some kind of…"

He interjects before she can finish her sentence, "Yeah, yeah! I know what a photo booth is. I just can't see what's so exciting about it."

"Oh, come on!" May Sissy pleads.

She is jumping even more with enthusiasm while he's trying desperately to get warm, but not succeeding.

Martial finally concedes to her demands, "Okay, okay. I can't take the cold any longer anyways. It's colder than a witch's tit!" They then start walking toward the mini-market.

11
Picturia

Martial and May Sissy walk inside the mini-market which is quite a spacious place for a mini-market. It seems at first glance almost deserted, except for an elderly lady — who is finishing paying for her groceries — standing before the first cashier just inside the entrance, while a newly hired employee, wearing a red apron, bags the groceries. Not far behind are two employees who are restocking the shelves with new products that they have brought out in a wheeled cart. At the same time, they are pulling old stock and putting it in their cart. There is the over-the-counter pharmacy department in the back corner of the store. In front of each of the five cash registers at the front of the store is a brand-new Silverstone light green and yellow round pot about the size of a Nivea Cream jar. They just came out in the market and are displayed on little stands set before each cashier's counter. The least that can be said is that the mini-market isn't stingy with lighting, for Martial and May Sissy are almost blinded by the — excessively — generous outpouring of the neon lights installed all around the store. They are bathing the place, or rather drowning it with a garish but nevertheless welcoming golden light.

Near the entrance is a splendid three feet wide little photo booth called Picturia.

May Sissy leads Martial to the booth while saying buoyantly, "Come on! It'll be fun!"

Martial and May Sissy walk toward the photo booth and get inside the tiny booth. May Sissy closes the red curtain behind them.

12
The Time Machine

May Sissy and Martial are both inside the photo booth. Martial feels cramped in this tiny cabin.

"Okay... Now what?" (Meaning: Okay, what are we doing here like two idiots?) Martial asks.

To which May Sissy says, "Wait, wait." Desperately digging inside the pocket of her coat, she finally finds what she's looking for in her coat pocket.

"Ah-hah! Finally, I knew I had one somewhere!" May Sissy exclaims victoriously. It's a coin.

She slips the coin into the coin slot while Martial looks at her with a dumbfounded expression on his face. He then asks, "What are you doing?"

While sighing deeply, she says, "Guess." She then adds with a sarcastic tone, "Don't you see? This is a time machine! So, which time do you want to travel to for a dollar?"

He chuckles while saying, "Hah-hah! Very funny!"

May Sissy, slightly amused, says in a light tone, while teasing him, "Hey, you started it first, genius!"

To which Martial responds, "Okay, my fault. Happy? Now what?"

"Now it's time to forget all the stupid poses we were forced to make on those boring family photos. On my count just be free and go crazy!" May Sissy says, as she's pressing on different buttons, trying to act serious and concentrate.

13
Leave your sins on the landing!

May Sissy and Martial stroll along Rusty Street. Martial walks his usual gait. His leather shoulder bag bounces against his side like a postman making his daily rounds. While May Sissy seems to let herself be carried off by an invisible wind. A 12-and-a-half-year-old shell of unconditional good vibes. Imbued with oozing freedom. With this inspiring, unapologetic buoyancy, an unquenchable thirst for life, enjoying the elements surrounding her.

Rusty Street is almost exactly the same, except that there is no pharmacy, but a quiet house similar to the remaining houses. May Sissy stops right outside her house. There are three marble steps that lead to the front door to which is nailed an imposing black cross. There is a sign on the door in silver metal letters that clearly reads, *"Leave your sins on the landing!"*

At that time, few people had cars in Rocky Tank Town, so it is quite normal to see Rusty Street totally devoid of the four metal wheeled horses. However, it gives the street a certain charm, untouched by modernization.

May Sissy says to Martial, "So, tomorrow morning at seven, okay?"

"Yes, okay. Even if I keep saying that your plan will never work."

Back then, Martial already had the look of a disillusioned worn-out man.

"And I'll keep telling you that it will work. As long as you don't forget." May Sissy retorts. "Don't forget what?" he asks.

"To bring your optimism along with you, silly!" she responds.

To which he says without conviction, "Uh, yeah."

She is about to climb the first step when she realizes he is staring blankly at the cross and the writing on the door.

"It's quite ironic," he comments.

"What? What is ironic?" she says, taken aback and rather intrigued.

Martial's look is blank. He looks at her, although it seems that he's looking through her... into emptiness... and says, "I lock myself inside my bedroom to keep away from the daily hell that is this world, whereas you lock yourself outside to flee from yours."

She turns around and moves close to him. She stops and stands right in front of him and says in a sweet voice, her nose pink with the cold, "I almost forgot." While she clutches her schoolbooks against her chest with one hand, she digs her second hand inside the pocket of her coat and fishes something out. She gives it to him and says with a sincere, touching smile, "Happy birthday!"

She looks at him. Her eyes like diamonds, deep and mesmeric, can cross the impassable barriers of the mind to unveil the most mysterious secrets deeply buried within the heart. Just as she is doing right now with Martial. He stares at her with bewildered eyes. He feels unsettled by her beauty, but especially by the strength that emanates from her, her strong personality that fights day after day adversity personified in the person of her mother, Marcia Misniwill. *Where, how does she find the strength?* In her company Martial could almost forget that to others he is nothing more than a common Negro. He can even forget that he lived in this godforsaken and primitive hellhole.

May Sissy then goes toward the front door of her house, climbs the four steps, opens the door, turns around to look at Martial and says with sparkling eyes, "And don't forget!"

To which Martial says in a low voice while lowering his eyes timidly, "Yeah, bring my optimism. I got it."

May Sissy quickly waves at him before she disappears inside the house, closing the door behind her. Martial remains on the porch a little while, looking at the present she gave him for his birthday. He smiles, touched by the four small black-and-white vertical shots they took together in the photo booth. As he looks upon the photos, he admires all the wacky faces they had made together. They both look so happy, filled with the joy and innocence of childhood.

As a dog barks in the distance, Martial stays a moment longer in Rusty Street, standing in front of the house, holding the thin strip of pictures in his hands, looking successively at the photos one after the other and at the metal sign on the door that reads, *Leave your sins on the landing!* And then says to himself in an almost inaudible voice, looking slightly dejected,

"Yeah... is being black a sin? That's the real question though."

He looks at the four pictures occupying the left half of his field of vision, while the right half is invaded by the front door with its imposing cross followed by the sentence. All forming a sort of artwork inspiring the title, *Leave Your Innocence and Carelessness on the Porch.* The innocence and carelessness sharing the same space with intolerance looks like two presidential candidates warmly shaking hands in spite of themselves, during a televised debate, all in the name of decorum.

14

NOVEMBER 21, 2012

Martial has now left the center of Rocky Tank Town and is now on Rusty Street just outside the drug store where May

Sissy and her mother used to live. He's looking at the same four photos on the left half of his field of vision, the right half being now occupied by the drug store. The 'artwork' no longer has quite the same meaning without the dualism.

The drug store is closed and due to open again the next day at seven thirty a.m. The drug store cannot be compared to those found in larger cities, yet it has nothing to be ashamed of compared to its competitors.

Twilight is at its zenith, blanketing Rusty Street with a tapestry of colors — its beautiful crimson, is turning to orange, covered with pale yellow bands. This mesmerizing celestial beauty looks like the work of Nyx herself.

However, Martial does not seem to admire the beautiful twilight which bathes his somewhat ghastly visage in orange light. No. He looks more like a wandering weary ghost, a hollow human-shaped silhouette.

He briefly turns his head toward the entrance of the town, and just for a very brief moment it looks like he is about to run away. Flee this place.

But he doesn't.

What is the point of running from the Past? When your Present is mirroring it...

His eyes maintain the same penetrating, distant gaze. He seems to be lost... very far from here... at remembrance doors...

15

SEPTEMBER 16, 1968
The front door opens and Martial walks in after he had walked May Sissy home. The door leads into a charming perfectly

arranged hallway about thirteen feet long, which ends at the staircase to the upper floor. Immediately to the left is the kitchen with an open doorway. The living room, only five feet away, has a glass door with a white wooden trim.

Martial has barely taken a step in the hallway when the floor begins to creak, almost immediately followed by his mother's blunt voice coming from the kitchen, "Is there a sign on our door that says barn?"

Martial's mother, Mindy, is only twenty-nine years old. She has never had to raise her voice to instill fear in her son. The mere tone of her voice was enough to garner respect. She was one of those young women able to demonstrate infinite goodness and tolerance, but she was also able to set boundaries and enforce them occasionally. Inasmuch as she had a good — sarcastic — sense of humor, that exact same wittiness of hers at times could prove to be a double-edged sword.

Martial stops short and asks, "What?"

He turns his head toward the kitchen, his mother's back is to him, but her head is slightly turned toward her son. She's wearing a kitchen apron around her slim waist and she is stirring a pot with a large wooden spoon. The kitchen is neither too small, nor too big; it is just the right size for two people. At first sight, it is a warmly lit room with perfectly well-fitted and comfortable design, right out of a Walt Disney film. Except that here, fairies or friendly helping animals are nowhere to be found. Set in the middle of the kitchen is a rectangular table with two wooden chairs. A beautiful orange-hued twilight filters through the window and accentuates the rustic aspect of the kitchen.

"Oh, I'm sorry. I didn't make myself clear enough. Is there a sign on our door that says barn?" retorts Mindy in a severe, authoritative voice.

Martial doesn't see what his mother's getting at and says, "No! Of course not!"

"Of course not! So, would you tell me why you still wearing your dirty shoes in the house?" his mother retorts. "That's because I raised a pig for a son!"

He lowers his eyes and realizes that he has once again forgotten to remove his shoes before he walked into the house. Not that his shoes are covered with mud, but he has been outside all day long.

"Sorry, Mom." As he looks down in shame. "But how did you know? You were looking away when I stepped in?"

To which she says, "Oh. I didn't know. I just guessed," taunting him in her naturally sly manner.

Markedly upset, Martial replies, "Hey, that's not fair!"

Losing no ground, Mindy says, "Yeah, I agree. But I was right!"

"You got me. But it's still not fair!"

She turns toward him, while holding an aluminum bowl in one hand and a large wooden spoon in the other.

"Absolutely! But what are you going to do about it?" she says teasingly while giving him a tender and understanding smile. He smiles back at her and is about to go up the stairs, when his mother calls him once again, "Hey! Aren't you forgetting something?"

Martial stops, turns around and looks at her impatiently and asks, "What?"

"Oh! So now I'm not your mother any more? I don't deserve a kiss from my little boy, huh?" Martial obeys and moves close to his mother. He kisses her tenderly on her left cheek. "Well, better than nothing," she says only partially satisfied. She immediately presents her big wooden spoon to him, so he can taste what appears to be a homemade Bolognese sauce.

Martial tastes the sauce, while his mother awaits the verdict.

"Hmm! Delicious as usual!"

He has barely finished his sentence, when he walks away, fearing that his mother might try to make him taste some more food.

Mindy looks at him, amused and says: "Yeah, you better."

16

Martial opens his bedroom door and goes into the room. He closes the door quietly behind him. Immediately on the left wall, is a cherrywood wardrobe closet sitting in the corner. His room should actually be called a museum for it is indeed stacked with all kinds of objects from floor to ceiling. Another dresser made of the same cherrywood stands in front of the bed with a record player on top of it. Just above it, pinned on the wall, is a huge black-and-white poster of Chuck Berry performing his famous *duck walk*. Beside the record player is an enormous pile of records creating quite a collection. The first record is *Apache* by The Shadows. Next to the wardrobe is Martial's desk which is packed with even more items than the dresser. A lamp sits on the right side while the rest of the desk is filled with books, papers and other knickknacks. There is a pencil cup filled with all kinds of pens and pencils of all colors which has an Elvis Presley sticker where he performs his devilish dance of *Jailhouse Rock*. The desk is filled with paper (containing schoolwork, mathematics etc...) and an impressive history book, which is opened to a page with a photo showing the atomic bombings of Hiroshima and Nagasaki. A simple wooden shelf is just above the desk.

There's a row of books on the shelf, such as: *The Shrinking Man* by Richard Matheson, *The Sign of Four* and *The Five Orange Pips* by Arthur Conan Doyle, *The Raven* by Edgar Allan Poe, *The Strange Case of Dr. Jekyll and Mr. Hyde*, *Treasure Island* by Robert Louis Stevenson, *A Clockwork Orange* by Anthony Burgess, *Dracula* by Bram Stoker, *The Tragic History of Hamlet, Prince of Denmark* and an *Encyclopedia of Greek and Roman Deities*.

A sticker with four black-and-white photos of Elvis in four different postures from *Jailhouse Rock* is taped right above the corner of the shelf devoid of any objects, thus giving the funny illusion that four little Elvis are standing on the empty shelf.

On the wall to the left is yet another gigantic poster of the film *The Shrinking Man* with a tagline that says, '*A fascinating adventure into the unknown!*'

On the nightstand next to the bed are — in addition to the bedside lamp and alarm clock — a Bible and a book entitled *The True Story of Christopher Emmanuel Ballesteros* by Maxwell Anderson.

Martial puts his bag and his hat and coat on the chair by his desk. He reaches into his bag and takes out his birthday present. He turns and flips on the record player, which already has a disc on it. And as the galvanizing first drum sounds from Apache are playing, Martial lies down on his bed. Above the bed, a crucifix hangs on the wall. He religiously enjoys the music — *Ah, Music! So delightfully addictive! Such a transcendental experience! Each new time, each new listening feeling like a mind-blowing trip* — while looking at the four photos of him and May Sissy. And while he's lying there, we discover the gigantic poster of The Shadows on the ceiling (The same photo for the cover art of *The Shadows by Themselves* by Royston Ellis with The Shadows. Consul Books. 1961). Martial stays there contemplating the empty space beyond the poster, still holding in his hands the strip of four photos and savoring every note from the *Apache* album. It is sweet perfection, a wild musical ride bewitching his ears. Perfectly content, he's closing his eyes to enjoy this moment of bliss even more.

    He eventually reopens his eyes and turns his head slightly to the night table on which rests the book *The True Story of Christopher Emmanuel Ballesteros* (by Maxwell Anderson). He clumsily grabs it with his right hand. He briefly contemplates the book cover and then removes the bookmark to replace it with the vertical strip of four photos. Not only is it a lovely time-capsule-like birthday present, but it also functions as a bookmark and a morale booster. He looks one last time at the four photos now hidden between two pages, and then closes the book and leaves it on the nightstand.

17

SEPTEMBER 16, 1963 OREGON
Martial and his mother walk down the sidewalk in an old neighborhood mostly frequented by the black community, while an icy wind relentlessly whips around his ears and the rest of his face. Martial is ten years old. He is wearing a thick cap with four large stripes of red, white, navy blue and black and a pair of winter gloves. Mindy is wearing a sublime yet

conservative skirt suit ensemble with a white top. As Martial walks along with his mother, he glances around at the old neighborhood. Mindy casts a protective look of motherly concern at Martial as they walk past a group of homeless men warming up around a fire crackling in an old and dirty metal barrel. As Mindy and her son pass by the homeless characters, the men stare at them quite suspiciously, which makes Mindy uncomfortable. She keeps her eyes on Martial with the same look of deep concern.

They walk on past an old chimney sweeping company that's apparently been shut down a long time ago and whose faded sign simply says *'Chimney Sweeping Company'*. The poor business is now a shadow of itself. What is left of it is a crumbling old building with no tenant except for occasional homeless people, rats or kids playing scary Halloween games. Moldy old planks cover the walls and windows. Most of the windows are broken or covered with thick layers of dust. However, Martial's attention is drawn to an original old advertising poster stuck to one window. A tag line is written on the poster:

DON'T LET THE DUST SPOIL YOUR CHILDREN'S CHRISTMAS!

A drawing shows a little girl and a little boy in their pajamas standing in front of the Christmas tree crying for no presents are laid at its foot. Their parents look devastated because they forgot to have their chimney swept.

Martial and his mother pass by the old abandoned store and continue walking along. Martial, impatient and excited, asks his mother,

"Where are we going, Mom?"

"You'll see. Haven't you ever heard the word 'surprise'?"

"Yes."

"So, you're also aware that it loses its meaning if I reveal to you where we're going?"

"Yeah," says a very disappointed Martial. Then immediately, he pleads, "But can you give me just a tiny clue, please?"

"Hm! Funny you've mentioned the term tiny." Still teasing her son.

"Why? Why?" he urges.

His mother still walking quietly says softly, "Hmm, I don't know."

Martial, impatient, begs some more, "Oh, come on! Please?"

"Ah-hem." She says sharply, as she makes the gesture of closing her mouth as one closes a zipper.

Exasperated, he sighs, "Ugh!"

Mindy stops, lowers her eyes on Martial and says, "Okay, here is a riddle for you. If you can guess what is behind you, I'll tell you where we are going."

Martial thinks for a moment, and then tries to look over his shoulder but his mother stops him with a warning, "Ah-ah! Without cheating! No peeking!"

She's a little amused by the riddle game she is imposing on her son.

But, seeing her son hopping up and down with impatience, she decides to end his misery and tells him with a smile.

"Okay, here is a tiny clue. You'll find out where we are going by turning your head." Martial turns his head and discovers with amazement that they are standing in front of a small local cinema called the Magic Coil, currently showing Martial's favorite film, *The Shrinking Man*, whose large poster is displayed outside with the tagline that says "*A fascinating adventure into the unknown!"*

"Wow!"

"I wanted to surprise you. I bought them this morning on my way to work. So, what do you say?"

She shows him two tickets to the film.

"Thanks! I love you so much, Mom!" exclaims Martial, as he throws himself into her arms.

"That's what I thought," she says with a deep glow of happiness in her eyes. "Happy birthday, my little angel!"

Ring, ring, ring!

18

SEPTEMBER 17, 1968
Ring, ring, ring!

Martial is abruptly awakened by the ringing alarm clock.

Martial has difficulty emerging from his sleep, as he's clumsily reaching for the alarm to shut it off. He slowly opens his eyes, rises and turns off the alarm clock which shows 6:45 a.m.

"Damn alarm clock!" he grumbles, rubbing his face.

Martial sits up on the edge of the bed for a moment, craving to go back to sleep immediately. But instead says to himself, "C'mon… Get up Martial. Get up!"

He remains seated on the edge of his bed for a while. Through the window, it can be seen that the sun has not yet risen.

19

NOVEMBER 22, 2012
Martial's reflection appears in the mirror of the medicine cabinet as he washes his face over the sink. His face is a little

pale and pasty with graying facial hair regrowth. Martial wears a large gray t-shirt with short sleeves.

The bathroom is entirely painted in bright white. A white towel is folded perfectly and placed on the towel stands. Everything is stored with care and precision, because even though Mindy is tolerance personified, the one thing that she can't tolerate is people who are slovenly.

Martial finishes rinsing his face and immediately grabs the towel. His face reappears behind his white towel while he contemplates his reflection, staring at himself as if trying to get in touch with his own subconscious. Despite all these years Martial has retained this wounded, blasé look. Even in the morning. '*Jeez! Would it kill you to smile once in a while? Or is the world that unworthy? Yeah, that must be it.*'

Suddenly, he is struck with the pain of a migraine. He opens the medicine cabinet before him and rummages through three small shelves, looking for something to calm the migraine, but much to his disappointment there is no medication apart from a simple cough syrup on the middle shelf.

"Shit!" he exclaims as he holds his aching forehead.

On the top shelf is a box of cotton swabs and a jar of Nivea cream, while on the middle shelf is a small bottle of eye drops and the cough syrup. Finally, there is a small blue box with dental floss on the top shelf. Martial looks at the ceramic pot on the edge of the sink with a toothbrush and whitening strips and says to himself in a slightly amused tone, "No wonder her teeth are whiter than mine!"

As he closes the medicine cabinet, Martial lets his mind wander back on memory lane... Martial stares into the mirror, nearly looking through the glass. His mind drifts to the memory of him and May Sissy walking on Rusty Street, toward the entrance while the sun begins to appear on the horizon before them. He's blankly staring at the mirror, staring at this hazy vortex, momentarily bridging Present and Past...

20

SEPTEMBER 17, 1968
Martial and May Sissy walk in Rusty Street toward the entrance to Rocky Tank Town while the beginning of sunrise appears like a subtle gradient in the horizon with a mineral blue resting on lavender blue, followed by blood orange complemented with subtle yellow flowers of sulfur. They're walking through the light morning mist which appears like a fine mosquito netting covering Rocky Tank Town. The way they walk is somewhat reminiscent of two cowboys, Calamity Jane and Wild Bill walking toward this eternal sunset. They move toward the entrance where they are supposed to take the only bus that stops just twice a day, in the morning at seven a.m. and in the evening seven p.m., to spend a pleasant day in Wyoming, somewhere far away from *Shitty Tank Town* or *Rocky Stank Town*, as May Sissy so delicately puts it.

    Despite the magnificent sunrise that announces the day — bringing hope with its sweet warmth, accompanying him in the early morning — somehow a rather persistent, almost imperceptible ounce of 'spoilery', misty *je ne sais quoi* alas foretells of a new winter-like day. However, today Martial is not the only one to bring a hat. May Sissy is wearing one too. However, hers is up much higher on her head than his hat is on him, strangely accentuating her beauty and natural grace. She has a perfect and beautiful braid swinging as she walks, for even though she did not inherit her mother's beautiful golden blond hair; May Sissy has no reason to be jealous.

Martial wears a plaid flannel shirt accompanied as usual by his beloved leather bag hanging from his shoulder.

"You intend to do your shopping with this?" she says to him teasingly.

"No. I'm just used to taking it with me. Anyway, I'm telling you that it won't work. I'm telling you. You'll see. Believe me."

"Stop being so paranoid! He won't throw you under the bus while driving. Don't worry. Trust me," May Sissy retorts.

As they arrive at the bus stop — which is located to the right of the entrance, on the corner of the road that also eventually passes by the secondary entrance on Raven's Feather — so does the bus. It is a rather rickety old bus — like a school bus — that must have once been a bright green, now faded and chipped.

"For that to happen he would have to let me put a foot inside the bus first," says Martial with his inimitable prematurely blasé, sardonic tone of voice; which May Sissy secretly finds quite endearing, cute, attractive even. Martial has barely finished his sentence when the front door of the bus suddenly opens before them and Martial discovers that the driver is a thirtyish-year-old Black man.

Martial is taken by surprise and slack-jawed. His round eyes are fixated on the driver. He looks on incredulously, motionless before the steps of the bus. The bus driver then speaks abruptly, but not without some lightness in the tone of his voice,

"So you intend to stand there until I became white or what?"

"Oh-uh, s-sorry," says Martial as he gets into the bus hastily. "About time!"

As soon as May Sissy and Martial climb on the bus, the

front doors of the bus close abruptly making a loud, agonizing metallic squeak.

21

They stand in the front of the bus and realize that the bus is empty. The bus driver then says humorously,

"Put your white and black butt anywhere you want. As you can see, we have some… room."

Once they finally take a seat, the bus takes off.

22

The bus pulls over on a street a little before the bus stop in the small town of Douglas, in Converse County. The front doors of the bus open and May Sissy and Martial exit.

Before closing the door, the driver informs them, "Don't forget, kids, seven p.m. or you'll stay here until tomorrow morning. Good luck with that!"

"Yes, thank you, sir," says May Sissy very politely.

Then the bus drives away, leaving May Sissy and Martial on the sidewalk.

23

Martial and May Sissy are sitting comfortably in a movie theater, sharing a large bucket of popcorn, while enjoying a double feature: *Tarzan the Ape Man* by W.S. Van Dyke, followed by *Psycho* by Alfred Hitchcock. The room is half filled, mostly young adolescents trying to escape from their boring and monotonous daily, just like Martial and May Sissy.

24

Martial and May Sissy are now coming out of the small local cinema. Once outside, as she puts her hat on, May Sissy can't help but express a profound disgust at one of the two films they just watched, as she says acrimoniously, "What a rip-off this Tarzan film was! Yeah, let's go in the jungle, piss off some animals and shoot like cretins at everything moving, including some poor helpless hippos! Or let the blacks fall into the void and die without reacting!"

She then mocks the dialogue in the movie, "Do not lose your nerve. We're all right." May Sissy continues with her tirade-like critique, "That's for sure, she's all right! It shouldn't happen much to her, he has his hands stuck to her ass throughout the entire trip! And that lazy Jane barely capable to move her lazy ass even to grab a damn rifle lying just beside her! She has to go bothering one of the poor blacks already busy rowing!" She then imitates Maureen O'Sullivan as Jane Parker in a deliberately ridiculous tone, *They look just like catfish on a rainy day. Riano, gun.*

Then she mimics Riano's role talking in an African accent, *Yes, bwana, yes bwana!*

"You seem to know the dialogue by heart," teases Martial.

"Ugh, please! What dialogue are you talking about?" retorts May Sissy with contempt.

Martial adds, "You forgot the part with Tarzan and Jane."

Which is enough to fuel the May-Sissy-locomotive who's already continuing her passion filled diatribe, "Oh yeah! Let's see."

She then imitates again Jane Parker in the same deliberately ridiculous tone, *'Thank you for protecting me!'*

Then Tarzan said, 'Me?'
Then Jane said, 'No, I'm only Me for me.'
Then Tarzan said, 'Me.'
Then Jane replied, 'No. To you, I'm you."

May Sissy now points at herself, imitating Tarzan, *"You."*

Martial walks on and says, "The film is getting old now. It was a different time. It may explain the racist aspects of the film."

Martial then realizes that May Sissy stopped walking and is still standing behind him, looking with a doubtful look. He stops and asks, slightly taken aback, "What?"

"Wait! I believe that tears are trying to seep from my eyes for your speech was so moving!" says May Sissy, teasing Martial gently.

"Oh, stop kidding me," he says in his usual quiet, almost absent tone.

She suddenly has a more serious, mature look, much more concerned as she says, "Nah, honestly, you really believe what you just said?"

Martial doesn't answer. He stares blankly at the floor and walks on. The sun disappears slowly to be reborn through dawn. The orange light of dusk covers his face.

May Sissy looks away and says unapologetically sincere,

"A generation's ignorance should not be a valid excuse. You should let go a little from time to time. Sometimes it almost feels as though I'm black and you're white."

"Perhaps because it is easier to let go when you know you're the right color," Martial says. She can't help but look at him with compassion, however, trying to avoid falling into any sort of pity.

May Sissy and Martial silently continue down the street, walking away from the cinema.

25

May Sissy and Martial are standing just before the secondary entrance at Raven's Feather where the bus driver dropped them off a moment ago, contemplating this splendid spectacle offered to them. The beautiful, spellbinding cornflower blue sky with a timid nuance of reddish-purple. The whole view forming a mesmeric work of art. A pure panoramic vastness of magnificence tinged with a hint of melancholy. The heavens offer May Sissy and Martial their perfect visual requiem-like Ode.

26

NOVEMBER 22, 2012
Martial closes the medicine cabinet. His pale reflection appears in the cabinet mirror.

27

Martial, wearing his coat, enters the living room where he discovers his mother, who's wearing dark gray pants and who's peacefully sleeping on the couch, while the TV is on low volume. The living room is dimly lit by the early morning light. Martial turns off the TV and approaches his mother and gently tries to wake her. Mindy emerges slowly from her slumber, opening one eye and then the other. She looks really tired and a little disoriented. It takes her a few moments to remember where she is.

"Uh-huh?" she mumbles as she wakes up slowly.

The best — and quite frankly, only — time to observe her vulnerability is during her waking moments. After then, it's too late, realizes Martial with slight amusement.

"You slept on the couch all night?"

"Uh, no. I woke up early. Too early, it seems. But where are you going?" she asks.

Martial replies as she sits up and leans on the armrest, "To buy some aspirin."

28

Martial walks out of the house, while pulling a cigarette from his pack of *Peace-pipe*; the logo is an Apache handing out a pipe as an offering with a poppy red background.

Standing now on the landing at the top of four small steps, he lights up his cigarette, and takes a puff, and looks away ruefully. He takes a drag of his cigarette again, looking up at the gray and shadowy sky when he suddenly hears a slight groan to his left. He turns and finds a brown adult American Pit Bull Terrier, with a white and red nose and a dark brown patch over his right eye, standing before the neighbor's door on all four legs, his pink ears standing erect, his short tail wagging frantically, his eyes fixed on Martial.

"Yeah, tell me about it," Martial says empathetically blasé.

The dog seems bored out of his mind in his pen. His little moans are rather heartbreaking, as he continues to fixate on Martial with pleading eyes.

"Don't look at me like that! I'm not the one you should take your day out on! Your owner should take your ass out once in a while."

He takes another drag from his cigarette, and says to the dog while swallowing the smoke, "Um, maybe you'll be able to answer this question that I've been asking myself for a while now. Have you ever seen the sun in that hole? Or is the big guy up there determined to piss on you?"

The dog just keeps staring at Martial with his big round eyes.

"Yeah, that's what I thought. Shithole sweet home, huh?" Martial says while taking a puff. There is a short silence, during which Martial wearily looks at Grand Street, lost in thought.

He then turns his attention to the dog again and says, taking a drag of his cigarette, "I bet you don't even know where your name comes from. Well, during the nineteenth century, England, Ireland, and Scotland began to experiment with crosses between bulldogs and terriers, looking for a dog that combined the hunting instincts, speed, and agility of the terrier with the strength and athleticism of the bulldog in order to fight bulls and bears in arenas or pits in fights to the death. So, that's where your name comes from."

The dog, still staring at Martial with his round eyes, cocks his head slightly, moaning faintly. The expression on his face seems to say '*Really?*'

To which Martial retorts, "Look it up on the Internet if you don't believe me."

He takes another drag of his cigarette while looking at the street with slight bitterness. The poor dog continues to watch him with innocent eyes.

"They snatch you from your natural environment, and supposedly domesticate you. Once they don't need you any longer, poof! Suddenly, you become a bother and they put you to sleep. You know you're considered aggressive and dangerous by the Marine Corps?" Martial says contemptuously as he looks blankly into the distance.

He swallows the smoke of his cigarette and adds, "Yet you're probably much less dangerous and stupid than they actually are."

The dog keeps staring at Martial tirelessly. Martial has just finished his cigarette that he immediately pulls another one out as he tells the dog, "You know what, doggy? You and I have some things in common after all."

The dog keeps his round eyes on Martial who lights up his second cigarette while saying, "Yeah, I know I should quit." He then takes a long puff and adds, "I had a dog like you once… He died."

The dog whimpers.

"Sorry, but I've buried him, if it's any consolation."

Martial inhales the smoke of his cigarette while his mind wanders far away. The first drop of rain begins to fall. Martial, with the cigarette in his mouth, slowly lifts up his head toward the gray sky. The expression upon his face seems to say, *'Here we go again!'*

29

View of Rusty Street from the sky, about fifteen feet high. The entrance of Rocky Tank Town is under a grisly rain fall and a glacial mist surrounds Rusty Street and the rest of Rocky Tank Town. An Alizarin Red Metallic MPV (like a SEAT Alhambra) appears at the entrance of the town. The MPV slowly enters Rocky Tank Town in the rain. Inside the MPV is the Swinton family. Coby Swinton who's driving, his wife, Julianne, and their fifteen-and-a-half-year-old daughter Polina, who looks at least seventeen. Given the massive amount of luggage — suitcases and boxes — in the rear of the vehicle, it appears that the Swinton family plans to stay in Rocky Tank Town for a little while. Coby Swinton is a fifty-seven-year-old man, about the same age as May Sissy, while Julianne is fifty-two. Polina is their only child. She wears a nice thick white fur coat. She looks out through her window and looks depressed upon discovering Rusty Street.

"No wonder you've left this shithole, Dad!" Polina says to her father.

"Mind your language, young girl!" says Julianne.

To which Polina retorts, "Sorry. No wonder you've left this horrible place, Dad!" She looks insolently at her mother and adds, "*Happy?*"

"Yes, much better. See, it's not so hard and you get to the same point."

"Whatever," Polina says, with the same hint of insolence in her voice. Polina is a splenetic, spoiled — little brat — teenager. She's basically an argumentative Living-Middle Finger.

"Don't worry. We'll only be staying here until the case sorts itself out," says Coby.

To which Julianne optimistically says, "It'll be a good time to take a break, far from the stress of the city."

To which Polina retorts, "Great." Then adds, "You guys couldn't find something else other than Creepy Tank for a break?"

She glares through her window once more and says, "Well, if I'm lucky I might get an autograph from Uncle Fester."

"That's the spirit," retorts her father.

The MPV moves very slowly on Rusty Street, heading toward the drug store, while the rain continues to fall over the Alizarin red metallic roof like a shower of gray ashes. The car pulls over, right outside the house next door. The MPV parks in front of the house. The pharmacy appears in the background on the right, and another house similar to the Swinton's house is on the left. Everything is immersed in this seemingly vindictive, unrelenting heavenly eulogy-like dark grisly rain.

The driver's side door opens, there is a long pause before Coby Swinton finally decides to get out of the vehicle. Coby opens the back door but Polina is reluctant to leave the vehicle and set foot in this capricious rain.

"Come on, let's go! What are you waiting for?"

"Are you kidding me? No garage?"

"Oh! I-I'm so sorry your highness! But no! No garage. Maybe a red carpet would make you more comfortable?"

"We don't even have a garage? Instead, we have to freeze our asses off under this pain in the ass! Oh sorry, I meant 'rain in the ass'," Polina says, as she steps out of the car reluctantly.

"Well, that's something you have in common at least. Now, help your mother, would you?"

Julianne, standing by the wide-open trunk can't help but press her hands against the car and smiles guiltily. Polina heads to the trunk where her father hands her a red wheeled suitcase while he takes several bags and starts to head to the house.

"What's the point of having so much money if it's to end up in this godforsaken hole?"

To which Julianne replies, "Well, maybe to offer you what you are wearing right now on your shoulders, Miss

Ingratitude!"

"Yeah, yeah. Whatever," retorts Miss Ingratitude.

30

Martial reaches the junction between Grand Street and Rusty Street, in which he is peacefully taking a walk. The rain falling doesn't seem to bother him in the slightest. Martial pauses in the middle of the junction and observes Rusty Street.

He finally crosses the junction.

He's now walking on Rusty Street, heading toward the drug store, next to which the Swintons' MPV is parked.

31

The drug store bell rings. The front door opens and Martial comes in. He sees the owner of the drug store.

It's May Sissy, now fifty-six years of age, standing behind the counter. May Sissy looks completely different from the young lively girl with sparkling eyes and energy to spare. She is no longer the girl who was always present to revive Martial's morale, often affected by the frustration that lived in him, emboldening his heart with her beautiful words. It often reminded him of the temperament of his own mother Mindy. The May Sissy that stands a few feet from him is sadly much more somber. She seems to be empty of the sacred flame that animated her when she was younger. She's still as charming as ever, but her eyes that were once full of life now have a cold stare, reduced to mere spherical witnesses frozen in time. It appears that a painful past has shaped her new personality.

May Sissy stands behind the pharmacy counter and looks

at Martial. There is one thing that remains the same about May Sissy; her now black hair is in a large and perfect braid, just like before.

Martial walks up to the counter, through a small and narrow aisle between two rows of products. The pharmacy is somewhat dark, as it's poorly lit. Paradoxically, each step toward May Sissy seems to take him away from the May Sissy he used to know. The closer Martial gets, the farther she seems.

When Martial finally arrives at the counter, he notices another change, which he did not when he walked through the door. May Sissy has become rail thin. Not that she was overweight as a girl, but now, under the low neon light, Martial realizes that she looks even thinner than she was in her younger years.

Smiling, May Sissy speaks to Martial in a straightforward manner, "Well, well, well. Been a long time, huh!"

Not knowing what to say Martial shyly responds, "Damn long! Yeah… too long."

There is a brief moment of silence, making Martial aware that not only has time separated them a little more with each passing year, it also sealed the memories in the depths of their minds. The only thing Martial and May Sissy share in this very moment is the same lost expression on their faces; visages belonging to two people who have lost sight of each other by forces beyond their control, each having had to face a life strewn with tragic moments that definitely changed them, fundamentally rewriting their personalities.

Finally, May Sissy breaks the ice, talking in the same straightforward voice, this time with a charming smile that briefly revives the May Sissy from the past,

"So, how can I help you? What do you need? Or, you've

just stopped by to say 'Hi'?"

"No, no, I, I mean yes, of course but I'm wondering if you have some aspirin, maybe?"

"What kind of drug store doesn't have it? I'll bring you that," she says while disappearing in the rear of the drug store.

"Thank you," Martial briefly says.

While he awaits the return of May Sissy, Martial looks over the entire drug store. His gaze eventually notices a new brand of cough drops put on display on the counter. The package is a small clear yellow sack, containing twelve coated tablets of black licorice. He slowly reads what is printed on the package while he waits:

COUGH CALMERS
12 Licorice cough drops.
Throat Lozenges

32

SEPTEMBER 16, 1968

Miss Viviente stands at her desk facing her students, among whom are Coby Swinton and May Sissy sitting side by side. Miss Viviente is forty-seven years old, but appeared to be at least fifty-five. She's a woman who always appeared older than her age. It certainly didn't do her any good that she always wore an awful bun that may have been beautiful on another woman but made her look like an old grouch. Her clothes didn't help her case either. She wore a chestnut brown skirt accompanied by a white blouse with khaki-green stripes. She was a strict teacher, sometimes harsh but always fair.

"Well, who can tell me how many kinds of twilight there are?" Coby raises his hand excitedly.

Miss Viviente calls on Coby, "Yes, Coby Swinton."

"There are three kinds of twilight: Civil twilight, nautical twilight and Astronomical twilight."

Miss Viviente praises him, "Excellent, Coby!"

Suddenly, the bell rings, announcing the end of class.

33

May Sissy comes out of the school. She wears a long thick woolen winter coat with stripes of three different colors, arranged in a gradient from darkest to lightest — from brown to beige and pinkish beige near the cuff — thus forming a lovely gradation. Her beautiful long braid falls on her hood with the same gradient behind it, giving her the appearance of an Inuit. Her coat is closed by four clasps attached around four black buttons (each with two small holes in the middle). She holds some schoolbooks in her arms. She spots Martial standing by the entrance of the school a bit further away. He's standing motionless with his back to her, while all around him other students are running, heckling, and shouting, except for a very few who leave silently, clutching their books and notebooks against them like sacred Bibles.

The expression on May Sissy's face suddenly shifts from jovial to aversion as she notices the presence of Coby Swinton and two of his inseparable friends — Carl Denton and Maxwell Tate — walking toward Martial.

"Move out of the way, pinhead!" vehemently says Carl Denton.

While Coby Swinton knocks Martial out of the way with his elbow and says coldly, "Hey! The sidewalk doesn't belong to you, you know!"

"Sure thing, dude!" idiotically chimes Maxwell Tate. Coby and his two buddies then walk away, laughing in jest.

May Sissy walks over to Martial and stops right in front of him. Now that she's standing in front of him, she realizes that his eyes are closed, and he seems preoccupied with his own thoughts.

"What are you doing? What are you waiting for? Didn't you hear?" Martial realizes that someone is addressing him and opens his eyes.

"What are you doing? What are you waiting for? Don't you hear? You plan to stay there until they reopen school tomorrow morning or what? Come on Martial." She then adds with gusto, "Now, it's time to forget all you've learned and enjoy life!"

34
Elephant Graveyard

May Sissy and Martial continue walking away from the cinema while the sun sets, casting an orange light over the street. They arrive at the place where the bus had dropped them off in the morning, where they are supposed to wait. Sitting on the ground is a black man, playing the banjo, while singing a song — *Elephant Graveyard* — of his own composition. His classic black banjo case lays wide open just before him. Martial and May Sissy are the only spectators except for a few passersby who seem untouched by the lyrics. There is no coin in the guitar case. No one has stopped to listen to the artist. His stare is steeped in melancholy, the stare of a disillusioned former activist, drowning in his disenchantment with what remains most valuable to him, his words, his lyrics: the extension of his flickering violated dignity. This small tarry patch of captivity, cold and confined upon which he presently finds himself, gives him the feeling of being shut off from the rest of the sidewalk, and by extension, from the rest of the world. It is as if there were invisible chains linking him to the patch of asphalt, against his will, forcing him into a daily, monotonous captivity. As his cancerous self-deprecation increasingly spreads, insidiously whispering. With every passing day, he increasingly hates what he became, or rather what this world has turned him into. A rusty obsolete and discarded tool. A leper-like nomad architect of phrasal nonsense whose very presence is disturbing and repulsive. Nothing more than an ugly empty shell whose soul fades away a little more with each of these seemingly pointless recitals. Like vainly preaching a Homily for occasional wandering doves who for a brief moment perched on the window edge of a church with no soul inside. Words fall silent when the passion dries up. He became aware of it. He became aware of the fact that to the eyes of others, of some people, this ancestral heritage of his he's been — and still is with growing difficulties — trying to protect, just like others before him, is perceived as this repulsive purulent wound threatening to spread and infect them and everyone around them. He knows very well that his cause is noble, *of course it is!* However, the daily disdain weighs as heavily as rusty chains thrown into the sea.

And while May Sissy is lost in her thoughts, apparently listening once more to the song already stored in her hippocampus, the bus appears and opens its front doors with the familiar rusty clanging and screeching. The bus is still empty. Martial is about to get on the bus when he realizes that

May Sissy did not seem to notice its arrival.

"May? Come on!"

May Sissy then turns her own personal record player off and emerges. "Huh? Y-yeah, I'm coming. Just a second."

May Sissy delves into her pocket and pulls out her cinema ticket and some coins. She walks up to the singer, still sitting on the ground and looking up at her with surprise, leans down slightly and gently deposits her money in the banjo case.

Gratefully and affectionately, the singer says in a gentle voice, "Thanks, little sister."

May Sissy goes into the bus. The doors close behind her and the bus drives away.

35

SEPTEMBER 17, 1968

The front door opens, and May Sissy appears in the doorway, closing the door behind her as she takes off her hat. She walks down the corridor as she usually does and takes a quick peek inside the rooms along the way. The floor of the entrance hall, like the rest of the house, is made of old dark brown parquet covered by a long red carpet with patterns of beautiful pink cherries, forming a stripe on each side like two sumptuous frescoes. On the right is a wooden window door with two panels overlooking the lounge.

To the left is a long and beautiful curved staircase leading to the first floor. The walls are covered with green khaki wallpaper of a strangely baroque style. On a small rosewood table, is a large, slightly green, plate that contains the mail and keys. Next to the plate is an old brown rotary dial phone. Above the table, is a small wall painting of the Virgin Mary carrying the baby Jesus in her arms. He's wearing a simple gown that covers his lower body, and his little head is inclined in a loving gesture. The background is brown, while the contour of the Virgin Mary's head is chestnut brown. May Sissy's eyes rise to the left wall, where an old oval gilt wooden frame hangs. There's a black-and-white photo of May Sissy, posing with her mother. Both have a solemn expression on their faces. Despite this, Marcia's natural beauty is somehow accentuated by the black-and-white contrast of the photo, especially her mesmerizing gaze. Both are wearing long dresses with lace collars and their hair is packed into a low bun. They both carry a small wooden crucifix around their neck.

36

May Sissy, who has now let her hair down completely, is wearing an old white nightgown. She's in the bathroom brushing her teeth over the sink. In front of her is a rather old mirror, ordinary, just like the rest of the bathroom. The floor of the bathroom is made of small black and white tiles that are in a straight line and arranged to form diagonal patterns. All the walls are painted white. Located against the back wall (a little to the right of May Sissy) is an old white cast-iron claw foot bathtub without curtains. Opposite the bathtub, is an old cast-iron radiator that was formerly white, but now slightly yellowed. On the other side of the room, opposite the sink, is the toilet. Between the toilet and the wall is a small wooden cabinet with two little doors. The bathroom is equipped with two standard light bulbs. The first one is in the center of the room, suspended from the ceiling, connected to a switch on the wall. The second one is just above the sink. It has a pull cord switch and is the only one that is switched on right now. On the left side of the sink faucet is a simple white ceramic soap dish. On the right is a ceramic cup containing a toothbrush and a tube of amber yellow toothpaste. To the left of May Sissy is the bathroom door, wide open and overlooking the upstairs hallway. There's a rather narrow hall on the left ending twenty-one feet further on the top of the stairs. Just outside the bathroom, down on the right is May Sissy's bedroom. Twenty inches of wall separate May Sissy's bedroom from a small closet, while twenty inches of wall separate the closet from Marcia's bedroom. Most of the doors in the house have white doorknobs. The entire house has parquet floors, except for the kitchen and the bathroom. The wall on the right, however, does not lead to any room. The hallway is lit by an old oversize ceiling lamp in the form of a pink glass rose through which a soft yellow light diffuses.

May Sissy finishes brushing her teeth, when a sudden sharp pain forces her to hunch over. "Ouch! Owe!" she exclaims.

She slips a hand under her night gown and moves it up between her thighs. When she moves her hand away, it is slightly covered with blood. The pain persists, causing her to wince.

"Oh shit!" she says in shock.

She rushes to the small cabinet between the toilet and the wall. She quickly opens it. On the top shelf is a row of white towels arranged perfectly, one on top of another. Next to the towels is a row of washcloths stored in the same way. There are two packets of sanitary napkins on the shelf below.

May Sissy grabs one of the two packages.

May Sissy comfortably sits on her bed, writing in her diary, which has a brown cover. May Sissy's room looks nothing like a twelve-year-old girl's bedroom. Compared to Martial's bedroom, which is full of passion and color, May Sissy's bedroom is sadly dull. It's almost depressing with walls covered with old green-beige wallpaper that is almost dingy yellow and glaucous green, giving the room a murky appearance. Upon entering, immediately on the left, against the wall is a little dark — somewhat obsolete — wooden dresser that has two drawers at the top, one in the middle and two at the bottom. Then, is the bed made of solid wood. The bed is almost in the middle of the room, a few feet over to the left up against the left wall. Opposite the bed is May Sissy's desk and a simple wooden chair. Like most things in this room, they're made of solid wood and quite outdated. Whereas most girls hang posters of their favorite idols on their bedroom walls, stars like Marilyn Monroe, The Beatles and Natalie Wood, May Sissy has a small painting of Christ in the Garden of Olives hanging on the wall just above her desk. Her desk is that small that the very few objects on it suffice to cramp it. There's a cup with several pencils and a fountain pen. A silver-plated candlestick holder on the other side. A light bulb, hanging from the ceiling over May Sissy's bed, illuminates the room. The room has one window with two panes of glass, which is closed.

    Little drops of rain fall silently against the glass to their death.

    Meanwhile, May Sissy is sitting in her bed, on her fluffy

white blanket. An imposing wooden crucifix hangs over the bed.

She begins to write on a fresh white page of her diary: *September 17, 1968 Dear Diary, Today, I...*

38

May Sissy, still sitting in her bed, finishes writing in her personal diary. She then puts the movie ticket between two pages as a page holder and closes the diary.

39

Rusty Street is now fully plunged into darkness. Above it is a beautiful mineral blue sky from which rain falls, a silent rain with a heartwarming effect. The only light in the street comes from May Sissy's bedroom.

40

May Sissy is now kneeling on the edge of her bed where she recites the evening prayer, with clasped hands, while the lit candle sits on the wooden bedside table. Its light faintly illuminates May Sissy and her Bible lying on the night table.

"Our Father in heaven, hallowed be your name. Your kingdom come, your will be done, on earth, as it is in heaven.

"Give us O Lord, our daily bread, and forgive us our debts, as we also have forgiven our debtors. And lead us not into temptation, but deliver us from evil. Amen."

She then makes a sign of the cross, stands up, and blows out the candle, plunging the room into semi-darkness. She pulls away the bed cover and slips comfortably into bed, getting ready to fall asleep, lulled by the rain falling outside.

41

May Sissy wakes suddenly with overwhelming pain in the pelvis.

She cries out, "Aah! Ah-ah!" as she winces in pain, sitting on the edge of her bed.

She gets up and starts to walk awkwardly toward the hallway while a constant throbbing pain sears through her.

She makes it to the entryway of the bathroom and clumsily reaches for the light switch.

She finally finds it and turns on the light, but the bulb burns out instantly. "Oh! S-shit! Aah!" she exclaims.

She has no other choice but to move in the dark all the way to the sink where she turns on the second light bulb. May Sissy is now standing in front of the sink. She hastily grabs the cup containing the two toothbrushes and the tube of toothpaste and removes them from it. She opens the tap and fills the cup. She holds it and with her other hand she takes a small bottle of aspirin. She drops an aspirin into the palm of her trembling hand. The increasingly insurmountable pain in her pelvis and stomach makes her shake nervously, spasmodically.

She then sets the tube of aspirin back on the edge of the sink and swallows the pill with a sip of water.

42

SEPTEMBER 18, 1968
May Sissy emerges slowly and painfully from her sleep in a room flooded with morning daylight. The tube of aspirin rests

on the bedside table. May Sissy first opens one eyelid. Wrapped up in her cover she grimaces as she opens the other one, "Hmm." She sighs, "Ah!"

While blinking slowly to get used to the blinding daylight, she pulls the cover off herself. She straightens up and sits on the edge of her bed. Yawning, she lowers her head and realizes with horror that her nightgown is covered with blood. There is a big blood stain that goes from her groin to the bottom of her night gown.

"W-What? Huh?"

She grabs the hem of her nightgown soaked in blood and passes her hand along one of her legs. The horror on her face grows intense as she moves her hand up between her legs. Stunned, she says, "W-Ha-Wha-What?"

Finally, she decides to stand up and turn around to look at her bed, she discovers a large bloodstain in the middle of the bed, on the white sheets. "Oh, S-Shiiit!"

At that very moment, the church bells ring out, announcing the start of the Sunday mass. May Sissy turns her head instinctively to the window and says aloud, "Oh, Shit! Shit, shit!"

43

The mass has ended, and people are leaving church. May Sissy, wearing her coat and hat, her hair completely falling on her shoulders, is waiting outside the church, observing every person with a somewhat pallid expression on her face.

Despite the shining sun, the icy cold seems to creep into the air, forcing May Sissy to put her hands in her pockets while her nose becomes rosy. She stands a few meters from the entrance of the church and seems to be looking for someone. She seems a bit annoyed, impatient. Finally, Martial and his mother come out of the church. Martial sees May Sissy waving at him. He then briefly says something to his mother who nods her head while saying, "All right. But don't be late for dinner? And I mean it!"

He replies, "Yes, Mom."

Mindy heads toward Grand Street, while Martial goes to join May Sissy.

"Where have you been? You missed the mass! It's just finished," Martial asks.

"Yeah, I know," May Sissy responds in a hushed voice.

He feels something is wrong, so he asks her, "Are you all right? You don't look so good."

To which she replies, "Yeah, I'm all right. I'm just feeling little bit strange, but it's normal. Don't worry."

They remain motionless for a long time in front of the church until everyone's gone. May Sissy's gaze seems lost in the distance, contemplating a void beyond the facade of the church, an emptiness that only she seems to perceive. Martial watches May Sissy, hoping that she will say something, but when she doesn't, he takes the initiative to break the ice with a somewhat relaxed tone.

"You always talk so much?"

She emerges from her daydream and looks at Martial, puzzled, and she says, "Huh?"

He smiles and simply says, "No, nothing."

There is another moment of silence during which she stares blankly at the facade of the church.

"So? What's the plan?" asks a perplexed Martial.

May Sissy emerges once again from her daydream and asks, "Would you come with me to the store?"

44

Martial and May Sissy are now in one of the sections of the store, strolling quietly. However, May Sissy walks with her head slightly bent down, staring at the floor with that same livid look, a tormented expression invading her face. Suddenly, she seems like an adult, a brief glimpse of the woman she could become. Martial tries again to break this invisible ice wall between him and May Sissy, who unlike him seems to move toward nothingness.

"So, today is the big day, huh?" Martial asks.
"Hum? What?" May Sissy asks back.
"It's today that your mother comes back, right?"
"Oh, yeah, my mother," May Sissy says in a hushed voice.
"Are you sure you're all right? I mean, you…"
"Yeah! I'm fine! Okay!"
"I'm just asking. I worry about you, that's all."
"Well, don't," she says coldly.

Martial stops walking, catching May Sissy's attention and forcing her to stop, too. He then says, looking gravely into May Sissy's eyes, "I'm sorry but that's a feeling I can't manage. 'Cause it's what friends do. Worry about each other."

A tear begins to appear in the corner of her eye. It rolls down her cheek, leaving a long-wet trail on her face. Now she is overwhelmed with an intense feeling of gratitude. She then says as she wipes her face, deeply moved, "I-I'm sorry, Martial. I really am!"

To which he says, "Hey! You owe me no apology, okay! Like I said, that's what friends do. They worry about each other. That's what friends are for. And not just during the good times, but especially the bad ones."

These few words are enough to warm the tormented heart of May Sissy, to boost her somewhat bruised morale.

"So, will you now tell me what this is about?" Martial asks.

She sheepishly responds, "It's a bit complicated... you know..."

"No, I meant what are we doing here?"

A ridiculous expression appears on May Sissy's face as she says, "Oh!"

The atmosphere becomes uncomfortable and they both look at each other quizzically, feeling slightly ridiculous. Martial hastens to add, "But if you want to talk about it, it's okay with me you know. I mean whatever the reason is for your prob... blues."

"That's okay. I can handle it alone. Thanks."

"Anytime! So, what is this about?"

"An electric bulb burnt out at home."

While pointing at a clerk further down the section, Martial announces, "Oh! Speaking of which, there's a sales assistant over there!"

The sales assistant is making sure that everything is stored in its right place when May Sissy's voice reaches him.

"Excuse me?"

The sales assistant turns around toward May Sissy and Martial and says in a friendly voice, speaking with a Texan accent, "Hi! How may I help you?"

"I need to buy a light bulb, but I'm not sure which one."

"Ah, without the actual model it may be a little difficult to know which will work!" says the sales assistant, looking sorry.

May Sissy immediately takes the burnt-out bulb from her pocket and says, "Oh, no, no! I-I brought it with me! I meant that I just don't really know which one it is."

"Oh! Okay then! Perfect! Follow me!" the sales assistant says in a jovial tone.

He then walks briskly through the different sections of the store, while narrating the history of electric bulbs, like a living Wikipedia, "Yeah, that's the damn problem with this kind of bulb. You see, every time the lamp is switched on, it leads to overheating of the lamp filament since the intensity of the electrical current is greater in the cold filament. This is why lamps burn out mostly at the time of ignition. And not to mention the filament which is slowly evaporated over the hours spent at a temperature close to the melting point; it thins and eventually melts during ignition or breaks upon the first mechanical shock. Ah! Another annoying effect as well, the gases produced by the evaporation of the filament, condense on the bulb and gradually blacken the glass, reducing the amount of light produced by the lamp. Ultimately, only five percent of the energy from electricity is used for lighting, and ninety-five percent gets lost as heat. Because, I'm not sure you're aware, but the temperature of the glass of an incandescent lamp reaches almost 300°C! So careful not to set any fabric or cardboard, paper or wood directly on the glass, otherwise you'll get fire in the house for sure!"

Having noticed the Texan accent of the sales assistant Martial can't help asking, "Are you from Texas, sir?"

The sales assistant proudly says while turning slightly toward Martial but still walking quickly, "Damn yeah! You're from there too, son?"

"Not me, my mother."

The sales assistant stops in the light bulb section, looking at the light bulbs while holding May Sissy's burnt bulb in his hand and says, "Ah! Life brings us to some strange places sometimes, doesn't it? Ah, here we go!" He finds the right bulb and hands it to May Sissy.

"Thank you very much, sir." To which he jovially replies,

"Anytime! If you need anything, I'm your guy. And, call me Marty. Everybody calls me Marty, at least back when I was in Texas." He looks at the new light bulb in May Sissy's hand and adds, "The ideal would be to have one from the Livermore fire barracks."

"Why?" May Sissy asks, intrigued.

"Why? Well, the first reason is that she has been shining since 1901. I guess the brains of the White House must not work the same way! Know what I mean?" He then immediately adds a bit awkwardly, "No, of course not, you're too young."

45

Martial and May Sissy, holding in her right hand a small plastic bag containing the new light bulb, come out of the bakery. They are both eating a delicious stick of licorice.

46

God will save me!

May Sissy and Martial walk quietly down R. A. Minnesota Avenue. It's quite similar to Grand Street, except perhaps that the ground, black as coal, is in very poor condition. It has a lot of craters in some places, giving the impression of having been hit by a shower of small meteorites. The houses also seem dated, as if they have never been restored since the founding of the town.

It's late afternoon and the sun is about to set.

They walk with their mouths full of licorice and they pass by an old lamppost. The lamp is near the end of its life. It begins to crackle. It lights up a second time, and then crackles again, finally going off.

May Sissy and Martial watch for a brief moment, doubtful that anything will happen, and then shrug their shoulders as if to say, *never mind*.

They keep walking until they finally reach the end of R. A. Minnesota, leading to the junction between Grand Street, R. A. Minnesota Avenue and Rusty Street. Grand Street is on the right. R. A. Minnesota Avenue is on the left. Rusty Street is in front of them. They're about to leave R. A. Minnesota Avenue when Martial says to May Sissy in a slightly amused tone, "Hey! You know the joke about the religious guy who's drowning?"

She shakes her head. May Sissy and Martial cross over to Rusty Street. They walk in front of the sun, which is disappearing slowly into the horizon, hiding away behind the immensity of pines, while Martial starts telling May Sissy the joke, "So, there's this guy who is drowning in the sea, and a boat sailing nearby comes to rescue him. A sailor on the boat throws him a lifebuoy and shouts: 'Catch the buoy!' But the drowning guy answers: 'No need, thank you. I'll be okay! God will save me!' So, the boat sails away while the guy in the water keeps struggling for his life. A second boat shows up.

"This time a sailor throws a net, you know, those big nets they use for fishing. Anyway, he throws the net into the sea and shouts, 'Grab the net!'. But again, the drowning guy replies, 'No thank you, I'll be all right! God will save me!' The second boat goes away leaving the drowning guy alone. A third boat shows up and stops. This time a sailor dives into the water to save the drowning man. He swims to the guy and says, 'Hold on to me. I'll get you out of the water!' But again, the drowning guy refuses his help, saying, 'No thank you, I'll be all right! God will save me!' The sailor gets back onto his boat, completely drenched and annoyed. He sails away leaving the drowning guy there. Eventually the guy drowns. He finds himself standing before God and says, 'Lord, why did you not save me?' And the Lord answers, 'I sent you three boats, you moron!'"

May Sissy suddenly bursts out laughing loudly. Her laugh sounds sincere and natural. Martial says as they head for May Sissy's house, "I heard it from my mother."

"Your mother sounds really cool." A smile appears on May Sissy's flushed face, her sparkling eyes meet Martial's eyes.

47

May Sissy, lying on her stomach in her bed, is writing again in her diary. Except for her coat and hat, she's still wearing her clothes, a cute, blue jeans overalls, over a thin white turtleneck. When suddenly she's startled by a rattling sound from the front door. Instinctively, she turns her head toward the open door of her room. She sits up suddenly. The front door opens and then closes. Then she hears the voice of her mother, Marcia, in the entry hall, "May Sissy! It's me. I'm home!"

48

NOVEMBER, 22, 2012

Martial is about to leave the drug store when Polina suddenly enters. She lets out a deep sigh of exasperation. Outside, a downpour of rain falls on Rusty Street. Polina, who's still wearing her coat, appears to have been caught in the storm.

"Ah! It never stops raining here?" Polina says, drenched from head to toe.

Martial smiles and holds the door for Polina. He leaves the pharmacy, while the noise of the rain drowns out the sounds of Rusty Street.

49

As Martial heads out into the desolate storm, he adjusts the collar of his coat. Then he quietly walks down Rusty Street, like a lonely wanderer.

50

As the door closes, the little bell above the front door rings. Polina is slightly startled. She turns her head and looks out through the door. She is a little anxious. She continues to stand at the entrance, noticing that there isn't any lighting for the moment and the bad weather outside only accentuates the darkness. Polina rests a moment as she catches her breath. She appears to have run in vain to avoid being soaked. She then sees May Sissy standing several feet away behind the counter with the same low neon light. The neon light illuminating the aisle between May Sissy and Polina suddenly starts to sizzle. Intermittently, it illuminates the aisle, making it seem like death row.

With a forced smile, May Sissy says to Polina, "Hello! Can I help you, Honey?"

51

Martial is wearing his large Payne T-shirt with short sleeves. He's in the kitchen, getting a glass of water while holding an aspirin in the other hand.

Mindy has already started preparing the Thanksgiving meal. The kitchen hasn't changed. It is exactly the same as before, except perhaps for its tidy appearance, which in this very moment seems to have disappeared under an avalanche of dishes — clean and dirty — and other kitchen utensils. The kitchen is lit by a single rose shaped lamp, giving off a nice light with pink hues. There are things everywhere on the kitchen table. There's a large stainless-steel pot. Right next to it are several large chunks of pumpkin ready to go into the electric mixer, then into the stainless-steel pot. There's also a blue plastic colander filled with peeled potatoes.

Mindy is wearing the same white apron as before, which has three red pecking hens, all embroidered in red. She's sitting and peeling green beans.

Martial drinks water and says to her, "She's changed so much." He grabs a towel and wipes his mouth with it.

"That's because you remember her as the innocent young girl you once knew. People change, times change too... Poor child! After what happened to her, so young... To watch your mother and grandparents burn and to survive it can completely change a person." She pauses, and then adds in a saddened voice, "For some of us life can be a lonely pilgrimage."

52

At the counter, May Sissy gives Polina a small plastic bag containing medicine and says, "Here you go."

Polina definitely seems to hate this place she's in right now. She's not the least bit embarrassed to show her true feelings whenever the occasion presents itself, as in this very moment. She snatches the small plastic bag, gives May Sissy an icy glare and says: "Thanks." Her thanks, short and dry, sounds more like a dull insult than sincere thanks.

As Polina is about to turn around, something lightly brushed against her calves, making her jump and cry out of stupor while looking down at the floor:

"Aah!"

Polina realizes in horror that what just brushed against her calves is a cute little piggy belonging to May Sissy. Polina's expression turns into profound disgust, as if she had discovered a corpse lying at her feet.

"What is this, a pig? Ugh! Gross!" as she stares with bulging eyes at this — loathsome — creature.

Upon hearing that, May Sissy, in a passive aggressive, caustic tone that sounds more like a warning, says to Polina, "Oh! It sounds so naughty in your mouth, Honey. After all, he isn't as gross as that abomination you are wearing that you have the audacity to call a coat!"

Polina, true to character, gives an arrogant response while glaring at the pig, "It's not my fault if I like them better in my plate!"

She starts walking toward the exit, saying to herself, "Creepy bitch."

Polina is about to cross the exit door when May Sissy says, "By the way, Honey!"

Annoyed, Polina turns around to look at May Sissy and says, "What?"

"Have a good Thanksgiving, Honey," says the same passive aggressive May Sissy.

53

CHEYENNE, WYOMING, MAY 1974

Several people are present for the vigil, gathering one last time with the coffin open. Lying peacefully inside is Aunt Anna, Marcia's older sister. She was forty nine years old, and she is endowed with a certain charm that is not diminished even in death. For even though she is lifeless in this very moment, we are inclined to wonder; Her beauty is such that it defies even the ravages of death... or perhaps the undertaker performed a miracle! Anna now rests in eternal sleep, with a peaceful expression on her face. Her pale hands are folded on her outdated black dress, just like the rest of the parlor.

The coffin is placed on a large old cabinet made of strong wood, covered with a large white lace tablecloth. A beige-orange candle is lit, so that it can guide Anna's soul through the darkness to salvation.

The layout of the house is similar to that of Marcia's house. The French door with two wood panels, which leads into the tiny living room, is wide open. The coffin is along the back wall, opposite the French doors. A little further on the left is a large window hidden behind heavy burgundy velvet curtains. In front of this window is a rectangular three-seat sofa, which has three non-removable velvet cushions made from the same fabric as the curtains. The sofa has a painted wood frame, which dimly reflects the golden bolts holding it all together.

The parents of the deceased, Neil and Stella Slatie, are sitting on the sofa. Neil Slatie is wearing a black suit and black tie. His hands are together and resting on his cane. He uses the cane not because of advanced age, but due to a serious injury to the right leg, which has left him dependent on the cane to walk. Stella Slatie, wearing a black dress, holds a white handkerchief in one hand. Neil, on the other hand, doesn't have the look of a grieving father overwhelmed by sadness. Rather, he seems distant and oddly stoic. He is a fervently religious man, who is accepting of death, when it comes for him or a loved one.

An elderly lady, who is over eighty years old, stands in front of the coffin for the last time before it is taken away. She has a serious expression on her face. Her hands are clasped close to her. Then she makes the sign of the cross. After she is done, she moves away from the coffin and goes over to the sofa, on which Neil and Stella Slatie are seated. She offers them her condolences, "My condolences," she says, holding Stella's hand and squeezing it affectionately.

Stella Slatie responds, "Thank you."

Neil Slatie adds with a tone devoid of emotion, like a mere formality, "Thank you for coming," as he shakes the old woman's hand warmly.

"Oh, but of course."

Then the old lady makes way to a young woman, barely forty years old, accompanied by her three children, two boys, one about four and a half years old, the other seven years old, and a three-year-old daughter. The three kids don't appear to really understand what they are doing there, lost in the midst of all these sad and somewhat scary faces.

"My condolences."

"Thank you," says Stella Slatie once again.

"I was Anna's neighbor. We were very good friends," adds the woman, moved, between tears.

"Thank you," says Stella, this time even more grateful as she shakes the hand of the young woman.

In front of the sofa, on the other side of the living room, stands a very old stately wood and glass cabinet. It dominates the room with its height. It almost reaches the ceiling. The walls are covered with simple yellow wallpaper that smells of sulfur while the floor is old and squeaky. The entire room is lit by seven glass bulbs on a large old black wrought iron chandelier hanging from the ceiling. A large crucifix hangs on the wall above the coffin.

May Sissy, now almost eighteen years old, appears timidly at the entrance. She wears a nice blue dress with lace collar, her hair in a low bun. She glances around in the room. Her grandparents, Grandpa Neil and Grandma Stella Slatie, are sitting on the couch. Anna's neighbor's young daughter is sitting next to Stella, when her mother says, "Come on, Sonia. Give up your place."

Sonia rises and gives her place to the old lady who sits down thanking Sonia and her mother.

"Oh, thank you, dear."

At that moment, while May Sissy looks evasively around the lounge, someone knocks at the front door. May Sissy moves toward the door in a graceful gait. As she moves toward the front door at a brisk pace, Marcia notices May Sissy's slightly pale complexion and fragile appearance, and bluntly tells her in an authoritarian tone as she's heading for the front door, "That's okay, I'll handle it, young girl, but stay right where you are."

She grabs the doorknob of the front door and she adds in her same authoritative, blunt voice, "I'm gonna need you for something."

"Okay," May Sissy replies, barely audible.

Whatever May Sissy gained in size and grace, she seems to have completely lost in personality. She is submissive and fragile, physically as well as psychologically. She already has the gaze of the fifty-seven-year-old May Sissy. A dead gaze of someone who has fallen on the path of perdition and desolation.

Next to the front door that Marcia opens is a metal bin with six umbrellas. Marcia opens the door and a distant cousin of Marcia is standing with his wife at the doorstep. The cousin, a fifty-four-year-old man of great size, stands in his dark blue suit and black tie. He closes his umbrella and says, with a serious expression, "Hey, Marcia. Sorry, we're late."

Marcia says nothing and simply opens the door a bit more to let her cousin and his wife in. They're a little soaked despite their umbrella. The cousin's wife warmly grabs Marcia's hand and says, "I'm so sorry."

Marcia gives them a brief nod, and from the way she and her cousin shake hands with a brief shake and without feelings, it is clear that she and her cousin are not getting along for some unknown reason. Marcia seems to avoid the gaze of her cousin and closes the front door while they head to the living room. Once she shuts the door, Marcia turns to May Sissy, still standing in the same place, her thin hands clasped against her dress, pale, shy and hesitant. Like a hesitant rabbit out of its burrow. Marcia, with her usual stern look, says to May Sissy, "May Sissy!"

To which May Sissy replies with a soft voice, "Hm? Yes?"

Watching Marcia's behavior with May Sissy, it is fair to wonder whether she has ever been a nun in a convent, because she sure acts as such.

Marcia comes up to her daughter, searches in a small pocket sewn into her dress. She brings out some money and gives it to May Sissy, saying, "You must go buy…" she then looks behind May Sissy at the rest of the living room. She appears to be counting the number of persons in the room. She sees her cousin and his wife greeting Neil and Stella Slatie, who are still sitting on the sofa.

"Eight candles, not sixteen, do not let him try to fool you into believing that he only sells packages of sixteen or any other lies. He sells them separately. I know it. So do you now. So, as soon as you get there, make it clear, and you won't waste valuable time! Understood?"

She looks at May Sissy, trying to make sure she understands.

"Yes. Understood," May Sissy says with the same soft voice, a little intimidated by her mother's authoritative coldness.

"Now, hurry up. We will begin shortly," Marcia says in the same calm but blunt tone.

"Yes," answers an expressionless May Sissy. Oddly enough, May Sissy appears to be much more mature, with a perpetual solemn expression on her angelic face, pale and pure. It makes her look like a responsible adult who faces adversity head on. Unfortunately, her cantankerous personality that yearned for freedom was her charm. It disappeared and gave way to gravity and this new personality, certainly more mature, but so unlike who May Sissy used to be. May Sissy immediately goes to the coat rack by the front door and grabs her long gray gabardine coat. She slips it on, putting the money in her pocket. She takes one of the umbrellas in the bin. On the wall just above her, there is a wooden console, on which there is a pink vase with a bundle of long-faded flowers.

May Sissy opens the door and is about to go out under the drizzle, when Marcia calls out after her, "Be careful," she says, more like a formality than from motherly love. Strangely, her words sound more like a warning than an advice.

"Of course," May Sissy says, opening her umbrella. The blankness of her face is saddening. Where is the twelve-and-a-half-year-old May Sissy? Sadly, the answer to that question lies with May Sissy herself, who closes the door behind her.

54

The night has just fallen. Holding her umbrella above her head, May Sissy walks along the sidewalk, a plastic bag containing eight candles in her left hand. The rain is slowly dying down, the last few drops die on May Sissy's raven-black umbrella.

As she walks, she looks to the window of a bookstore, still open. The first novel of an unknown novelist, named Stephen King, is displayed in the window. The novel is titled:

CARRIE — A NOVEL OF A GIRL POSSESSED WITH A TERRIFYING POWER.

May Sissy walks to the window. Her curiosity grows as she gets closer to the window. Her face is marked by intrigue as she examines the book. The illustration on the cover shows the left face of a young girl named Carrie.

55

The front door opens, and May Sissy returns to the house holding the small plastic bag in her hand. Meanwhile her mother is waiting for her and reproaches her while walking briskly toward her, "What took you so long?"

May Sissy takes a long time to answer. She feels stifled under the oppressive gaze of her mother, whose scowl is meant to say *'So? I expect an answer! What took you so long?'*.

It is almost possible to see May Sissy's soul escaping through her eyes at that point in time; a poor soul confined in chains from the moment she set foot in the house.

May Sissy finally manages to say, or more precisely stutter, in an intimidated voice, "It was crowded. I-I-I am really sorry, Mother."

Marcia's glaring at May Sissy as she grabs the plastic bag containing the candles and says, "You should be."

"I-I-I am really sorry, Mother," stutters May Sissy again.

"Yes, yes! I understood the first time. Now, put away your umbrella and go get ready. And quickly! We're about to begin," says Marcia coldly, without raising her voice. She doesn't need to.

"Y-Yes, Mother," says May Sissy as she puts her umbrella in the pot among others.

May Sissy — still wearing her coat — lowers her eyes and heads for the stairs located immediately on the left. The hallway continues on the right, then twenty-one feet further, it opens into the kitchen. Under the stairs is a wooden door leading to a very old cellar.

May Sissy reappears downstairs. She's now wearing a beautiful long blue dress of similar design as her mother's black dress. May Sissy steps down the last few stairs gracefully. She finally reaches the bottom of the stairs and walks to the living room.

The living room is lit by two candles placed on either side of the coffin as well as the one that Neil and Stella Slatie have in their hands. At the end is the elderly lady. They are all standing in a circle in front of the coffin with a solemn expression on their faces. Marcia is standing in the middle holding two candles, hers and May Sissy's. She gives May Sissy a stern look. May Sissy moves toward her mother and the other members. Marcia hands her the candle. May Sissy stands between her mother and Sonia, Anna's three-year-old little girl who looks at everyone with her innocent eyes, not knowing what she's doing among these adults with their solemn and somewhat ominous faces. May Sissy smiles at her, as if to reassure her. Standing in the same circle (left to right) are Anna and her seven-year-old son, followed by her four-and-a-half-year-old younger son and Sonia. May Sissy is standing next to her mother who's at the center of the circle. Next to May Sissy are Neil and Stella Slatie, Marcia's cousin and his wife, and the elderly lady. All, except for the three children, have a small wrought iron candle holder with a large white funeral candle. It illuminates their faces and the yellowish light gives their visages the same sepulchral expression. The seven-year-old boy seems to understand the reason he and his mother are here. However, his little brother and little sister, Sonia, look uncertain as they look at the spooky faces around them (scary and rather confusing for kids of their ages), not to mention the open coffin before them.

Marcia, standing in the center, as the master of ceremony, starts to recite a long prayer in a solemn and steady voice, "God our Father, we are gathered here to pray to you. Death struck us and took away the ones we love and left us with a big void in our heart and a painful wound. We now stand here with our distress, our pain our questions. Tonight, we remember the words of Jesus, 'I am the resurrection and the life'. We have our hope and believe that she who was taken from us now lives in your house and that one day we'll be reunited again. O God our Father, wipe our tears, comfort our hearts and make our hope grow until the day of reunion in your kingdom. Through Jesus Christ our Lord. Amen."

The rest of the circle responds in unison, "Amen."

"The cross of Christ governs our prayer. Jesus went through agony and death. He knows from experience what men must endure. We can turn to him and share his pain."

"Have mercy on us."

"Lord Jesus, who wept at the grave of your friend Lazarus.

"Have mercy on us."

"Lord Jesus, who was abandoned and left alone in difficult times of agony."

"Have mercy on us."

"Lord Jesus, who sacrificed your own life in the name of the truth."

"Have mercy on us."

"Lord Jesus, who entrusted our God with your own life."
"Have mercy on us."

"Lord Jesus who comforted your friends in spite of your

own sufferings."

"Have Mercy on us."

"Lord Jesus whom our father rose from the dead to give us hope of resurrection."

"Have mercy on us."

"Words fail us, Lord. We stand in the face of a challenge. Accept our silence as a prayer for our sister whom you know and love. Her path now leads to you. Welcome her into clarity and peace of your kingdom. May your love for us be light on the road until the day you will gather us near you here and forever. Amen."

"Amen."

Marcia stops for a brief moment and resumes, this time, reciting the Book of Wisdom 'Wisdom 1, 13-14a; 2 la.2-4. 23':

"God did not make death. He does not rejoice in the loss of the living. He created all things so that they remain. The ungodly are not in truth and reason as they themselves say: We are born by chance, and after our death, we shall be like if we had not existed. The breath of our nostrils vanished like smoke and thought is a spark that the beat of our heart. If it goes, the body goes into ashes and mind will vanish like a gentle breeze. Over time, our name will be forgotten and no one will remember what we were. They are wrong because God created man for an imperishable existence. They were made in his own image. Lord, our sister communed with your Son, in the suffering of sickness and hardship. She completed in the flesh what is lacking the passion of Christ. Allow her also to share the glory of his resurrection, who lives forever and ever. Amen."

"Amen."

"In these trying times, I beseech you, Lord, who cares for

our suffering. Before the mystery of death, do not abandon us. In this moment of grief and painful separation."

"Lord, stay with us."

"In this moment of sufferings, despair and fear."

"Lord, stay with us."

"That we keep the memory of our sister, in the hope of reuniting with her and with you."

"Lord, stay with us."

"Despite the suffering and hardship, our hearts know and thank God for all that we have lived through with our deceased sister, to whom we were so close and who left us, thank you, Lord.

"For the affection she brought to her family, thank you, Lord. For the happiness she poured around her, thank you, Lord. For the qualities we appreciated in her, thank you, Lord.

"For the example she leaves us, thank you, Lord. For the hope to see her again, thank you, Lord.

"In these days of sorrow and trouble, we are certain that the Virgin Mary is close to us. She has known the death of her Son and offered him in faith and abandonment to the Father in heaven. We ask him to be with us in these painful hours and help us live in the hope of the resurrection. Now we entrust to God, she who has left us. Let's pray together."

"Allow her O' Lord, to gaze upon your face. Allow her, O Lord to behold your face. After the joy and love that illuminated her life. After the pain and the tears that covered her eyes.

"After the sin that has marred her sight. Since the truth is righteousness in her conscience. Because she believed in you without having seen you.

"Lord, our sister now leaves her earthly home, leaving

behind the suffering of those who love her. Let us keep her memory, not in the bitterness of what we have lost or to only regret the past, but in hope of the Kingdom where you assemble us. By Jesus Christ our Lord. Amen."

"Amen!"

"Lord, we turn to you at the hour that one so dear to us has departed. Grant her entry into your Kingdom and strengthen our hope to see her with you again, forever and ever. Amen."

"Amen."

57

AUGUST 1974

The summer sunlight floods the room. May Sissy is wearing a white gown with her hair down. She's lying on her stomach on the white blanket on her bed. The bed is placed in the middle of the room against the left wall, above which the same large wooden crucifix hangs. She is completely absorbed in a book. Her room has barely changed and looks nothing like the bedroom of an eighteen-year-old woman. The same old depressing faded beige wallpaper covers the walls. On the left, against the wall, is the same dark small old wooden dresser. Above this small cabinet is a square mirror with a wooden frame. Most mirrors in a young woman's bedroom serve as a decorative object to admire oneself. May Sissy's is a very modest mirror. There are still no posters of The Doors or David Bowie hanging on the walls. The same small painting of Christ in the Garden of Olives is still hanging on the wall just above her desk. Classics never die!

In front of the bed is the same hardwood desk with the

same simple plastic pot filled with pencils and a pen, and the same simple chair in solid wood. The two-panel window is wide open.

A gentle summer breeze blows through the white curtains.

The same small candle holder and the same old worn Bible sit on her nightstand.

While May Sissy is delving into her book, someone knocks twice on her bedroom door and enters immediately without bothering to wait for permission. May Sissy barely has enough time to hide her book under her pillow and turn her head to see her mother. She smiles for the first time in a long while, illuminating her face, accentuating her natural charm. Marcia is one of those women who, regardless of the expression on her face, subjugates others by her natural charm. Whether she is smiling or not, it is still with the same disarming efficiency. Marcia still wears the same long black dress with a collar lace, her hair tied in a low bun.

Marcia says to May Sissy while hiding something behind her back, "Hey! Wonderful summer day, isn't it?"

May Sissy sits up in her bed and smiles at her. "Yes, indeed."

However, despite the suave and engaging smile, a strange and unspeakable danger is almost palpable in Marcia's eyes, a danger ready to emerge at the slightest provocation.

Marcia moves toward May Sissy; she glances at the old damaged Bible on the nightstand. She finally stops in front of the bed, as May Sissy looks at her warily, expecting the worst, because the worst is usually what accompanies the unexpected arrival of her mother, usually leaving behind a bleak atmosphere of desolation and solitude, like a bird of a bad omen. However, for once the smile of Marcia seems the sincerest in the world. It seems that today is one of those few days when Marcia's heart beats like other loving mothers. Marcia, for the most part, manifests unfailing authority and self-righteousness. However, she occasionally shows sincere maternal love, granted it appears as often as a solar eclipse, but when it does, it's all the more moving, because she is unaccustomed to showing her feelings. When she does, a strange expression appears on her face, feelings of doubt and uncertainty — that she represses deep within her most of the time— of being convincing in this role of a loving and concerned mother. That would be the equivalent of discovering that you can survive without breathing. There would be an adjustment period during which you'd be focused on your non-existent breathing and nothing else around you. That's sort of what Marcia feels like right now. It's not that she never cared for her only daughter; she did care, like all mothers. However, her love stops where her religious fanaticism begins. Surely, the *"Love one another"* of her idol did not have a big effect on her. Marcia stands in front of May Sissy, leans in toward her, while saying in a soft, calm voice,

"Happy birthday!" Warmly offering her a new Bible as a birthday present, she adds, "You didn't think that I had forgotten, did you?"

To which May Sissy, a little surprised, says, "No. It's just that I must admit I had forgotten that it's today."

Someone like Marcia, fumbling with her feelings, can't really discern when expressions are false, such as those being faked by May Sissy in this very moment. May Sissy's eyes are trying their best to tell the best lie possible while her mind on the other hand doesn't even bother and lets out a very loud and clear *'Oh yeah, my birthday! Now that I see your gift, I wish you had forgotten it.'* that resounds against the Marcia-free walls of her mind... So gratifying!

"I noticed that yours was beginning to get a bit old and worn out. That's not the best way to enjoy the Lord's words, is it?" Marcia says as she smiles softly at May Sissy.

"Right. Thank you very much, Mother. You shouldn't have. That's really kind of you."

In that moment May Sissy feels bad though. She feels like she took advantage of her mother's brief moment of vulnerability. Like she's betraying her. Sorrow and bitterness invade her body in a disturbing dance of opposites, of cold and warmth.

"Take good care of this one," says Marcia.

"I will."

Marcia leans toward May Sissy, puts both hands on her temples and kisses her daughter on the forehead tenderly while saying in a hushed voice, "My sweet little angel. I love you. I hope you know that. Don't ever doubt my love for you."

"Of course. I love you too, Mother."

Marcia straightens up, looking at her daughter tenderly. Then she goes to the door and leaves while May Sissy is still looking at her.

As soon as the door is closed, May Sissy lets out a deep sigh of relief. She then says bitterly to herself in low voice as she's looking down at the brand-new Bible she still holds in her hands,

"Happy birthday, May Sissy. Make a wish."

58

"Anywhere but there! Anywhere but there!"

May Sissy is wearing her open large long khaki coat, a dress and her ballerina shoes. She's out of breath, running like a crazed woman through a sea of trees. Frantically encouraging herself with this very brief Mantra-like motivational phrase, "Anywhere but there! Anywhere but there! Anywhere but there! Anywhere but there!" She runs without ever looking behind her. Her long hair hangs down with her leather bag around her shoulder and her coat open. She seems to be running the marathon for her freedom, for her very survival…

59

SEPTEMBER 1974
Returning from school, May Sissy opens the front door. She's wearing a long khaki coat with two wooden toggles fastened by hooks and a denim overall dress and ballerina flats. May Sissy seems to have permanently swapped her long braid for free-flowing hair that comes almost to the waist. Like her mother, May Sissy does not have pierced ears and therefore never wears earrings. She carries a broad leather shoulder bag on her arm. She has barely closed the door when she turns to see her mother standing in front of the entrance to the living room. She's still wearing the same long black dress with a lace collar, while her hair is packed in a low bun. She seems to have been awaiting May Sissy's return. Marcia then examines everything with her suspicious, piercing gaze. This looming calm before the storm. The warm smile completely disappears from Marcia's face, replaced by her favorite stern expression as she says in a pretentious monastic calm:
"How was your day at school?"

"Oh… It was fine," May Sissy answers, barely smiling.

"Oh! Good. Good," Marcia says, in the same pretentious monastic calm as she's smiling in a disconcerting manner.

May Sissy heads for the stairs and starts to climb under the pervasive gaze of her mother.

60

May Sissy, wearing her white gown with her beautiful hair down to her lower back, stands before the same old mirror, brushing her teeth. She rinses her mouth and spits everything into the sink. Then she raises her head. Her gaze falls on her reflection, as if for the first time. The expression on her face is that of the young twelve year old May Sissy meeting the beautiful young eighteen year old woman she has become for the very first time. As she's lost in her reflection, she suddenly feels pain in her chest, forcing her to press her hand against it. She massages herself mechanically while grimacing in pain. The pain slowly decreases but persists. May Sissy then unbuttons her dress and takes a quick glance over her breasts. For the very first time in her life, May Sissy wishes that she had a girlfriend to talk to. The female equivalent of Martial. She stares at her breasts and contradictory thoughts pollute her mind.

The bathroom looks exactly the same as before, except for a transparent shower curtain hanging above the old white cast-iron bath. The door to the bathroom is wide open on the narrow corridor. It's still illuminated by the same old ceiling lamp in the shape of a rose diffusing the same saccharine yellowish light.

May Sissy looks one last time in the mirror and groans.

She pulls the cord next to the mirror. The light bulb located over her head goes off, plunging the room into total darkness.

61

May Sissy stands in front of her mirror, rummaging through one of the sliding drawers from which she takes out a hairbrush. As she closes the drawer, a new pain takes her by surprise, forcing her to press her free hand against her chest. She massages her chest mechanically while grimacing, more due to annoyance than to pain. This time, the pain is less persistent and stops almost immediately.

May Sissy has never been the kind of girl to contemplate herself in the mirror. She never really took time to observe the gradual evolution of her body as she changed gradually but inevitably from a young girl into a young woman. The only change she ever noted was the appearance of her first and painful menstruation.

The brief chest pain resolves.

It seems that she's getting aware of it for the first time. She turns sideways and observes her silhouette. The drab yellowish light of the light bulb blends in with the beige—yellowish old wallpaper, accentuating its murky and depressing aspect. Creating a perpetual cycle of drabness with no end in sight. May Sissy stands facing the mirror and is about to untangle her very long hair with her hairbrush before going to bed. As she combs her hair, wincing slightly in pain, she suddenly hears a voice.

"Need help?" Marcia says in a very calm voice.

May Sissy turns her head instinctively, perceiving the presence of her mother, standing in the doorway, still dressed in the same long black dress with lace collar, with her hair still packed in a low bun. Her piercing eyes still having the same solemn expression.

"Oh, I-I don't want to bother you," says May Sissy in a shy voice, intimidated whenever she addresses her mother, carefully weighing every word she utters.

Marcia goes to the chair by the desk, as she says, "No. It's fine."

Marcia takes the chair and goes to May Sissy who is still in front of the mirror. She sets the chair just in front of the mirror, between the bed and the cabinet, and says to May Sissy in an engaging and ingratiating tone, "Come on. Sit down."

She gives her an unsettling smile. If Marcia had been an animal in another life, she was undoubtedly a hawk, majestic and formidable, with a keen eye, from which nothing could escape.

May Sissy sits on the chair without hesitation. "Very well," Marcia says.

Marcia sits on the edge of May Sissy's bed, just behind the chair May Sissy is sitting on. May Sissy is confused. *Is it the beating heart of her mother, sincere and loving? Or is it the mother superior persona with a poisoned chalice?* May Sissy wonders. *Do I have to fear a sincere, but so rare outburst of genuine affection that will end with a 'Good night, sleep tight!' accompanied by an equally sincere kiss on my forehead? Or should I fear this little calm moment before the storm, which will end in desolation and solitude?*

The reflection of May Sissy appears, her mother behind her sitting on the edge of her bed. This vision is not comforting. It accentuates the awful feeling of imprisonment that May Sissy feels daily. She has the surreal impression of seeing the picture lying in the entrance suddenly come alive before her, when Marcia says, "Now, shall we begin?"

"Y-Yes. Please."

There is a brief moment of silence during which Marcia seems to expect something, resting her gaze on May Sissy when she pretends to look away. Marcia then says calmly, "May I have the hairbrush?"

"Oh, yes. Sorry," May Sissy says, hastily giving her the hairbrush.

Marcia takes the brush and says, "It's all right."

Marcia gently begins to comb her daughter's long hair. As she combs May Sissy's tangled hair, Marcia begins to hum a French lullaby, *Les Petits Poissons dans l'eau*, which she used to sing to May Sissy when she was little.

"Hm-hm-hm-hm-hm! Hm-hm! Hm-hm-hm-hm, hm-hm-hm-hm-hm-hm-hm…"

Somehow, in this precise moment, May Sissy has a deep respect for her mother. Apart from her crazy fanaticism, she is a strong woman imbued with a profound and inspiring majesty and self-respect. May Sissy even entertains the thought of becoming like her. Tough, courageous, beautiful, a beacon of bravery against adversity. There is something tragic about Marcia. She is like a formatted android trying her best to go against the tide. Marcia is like a turtle with a faith forced upon her. Contrarily to what we would think she was in many ways like May Sissy. Like a remnant of a long-gone May Sissy.

Marcia's voice fills the room, like the voice of an angel…

62
Les Petits Poissons Dans L'eau

ROCKY TANK TOWN, 1960

Marcia wears her very long black dress with a lace collar. Her hair is tied in a low bun. She sits on the edge of four-year-old

May Sissy's bed, singing the French lullaby, *Les petits poissons dans l'eau*, with her soft voice while stroking her cute daughter's hair. Her sweet and innocent face is lit by a candle sitting on the bedside table.

Les petits poissons dans l'eau Nagent, nagent, nagent, nagent, nagent Les petits poissons dans l'eau

Nagent aussi bien que les gros

Les petits, les gros, nagent comme il faut Les gros, les petits, nagent bien aussi Les petits poissons dans l'eau

Nagent, nagent, nagent, nagent, nagent Les petits poissons dans l'eau

Nagent aussi bien que les gros

Les petits, les gros, nagent comme il faut Les gros, les petits, nagent bien aussi Les petits oiseaux, là-haut

Volent, volent, volent, volent, volent Les petits oiseaux, là-haut

Volent aussi bien que les gros

Les petits, les gros, volent comme il faut Les gros, les petits, volent bien aussi Les petits, les gros, volent comme il faut Les gros, les petits, volent bien aussi

May Sissy feels safe as she looks up at her loving mother. *No harm could possibly befall you. Not on my watch! I would rather look at Death's gaze than let something happen to you.* That's what Marcia's eyes say to the innocent May Sissy. Sometimes people find faith, sometimes faith finds them, sometimes faith is born out of love, sometimes out of fear. For some it is a revelation, an awakening, a (re)birth. That's how important May Sissy was to Marcia.

"What does that say?" May Sissy asks her mother innocently.

"It says…" starts Marcia. She pauses for a moment, trying to come up with a good way to translate it. "It is about little fishes peacefully swimming in the water and little birds flying freely in the sky."

"And then what happens to them?" May Sissy asks.

Locking eyes with May Sissy, Marcia tells her softly, stroking her hair affectionately, "Nothing. They just keep swimming in the water, and flying up there, sweetie."

POETIC INTERLUDE
ODE TO MOTHERHOOD

<u>MY SWEET LITTLE, LITTLE, LITTLE</u>
My sweet little, little, little Gift Do not be scared of the dark
Do not be scared of the night Just close your eyes
Free your mind And you will see The sweet smile Of your Mommy
My sweet little, little, little Angel My arms will always be your cradle My sweet little, little, little Baby
My voice will always be your lullaby Look at my eyes
While I look into yours
The entire world around us doesn't matter any more Only the love of each other... and nothing more
My sweet little, little, little Treasure I wish you the sweetest dreams
Make your dreams as you make my life Full of innocence
Full of your presence Full of perpetual sunshine
My sweet little, little, little Bird I will always be there for you
For your very first steps
For your very first word For your very first ice cream
As I have been for your very first scream
What you will go through I will too
From me you can always find some strength to borrow My hands padded with tenderness like a sweet pillow I will always be there to comfort you
My sweet little, little, little sunshine The Sun has no secret for

me any more
Happiness has a taste since you were born And my life has a purpose
Seeing you grow up into this world
For you, my eyes will cry
For you I will share my greatest smile
With a sweet kiss, your tears I will dry
My sweet little, little, little star It is time for me to close my eyes So, do not be scared of the night Do not be afraid of the dark
Because I'm gonna join you in your world Full of funny plush, toys and love
So, close your eyes now
Let yourself be lulled by the beats of my heart And let's welcome together this beautiful dusk Before enjoying the next wonderful Morn And when tomorrow will come
Do not be scared of the day Do not be afraid of the light Just open your eyes Gently, One by one
And you will see
The sweet welcoming arms of your Mommy

BRIGHT SIDE

Bright side... Bright side, where are you? Bright side... Bright side
Why are you so shy?
Help me to transform into a smile This deep sigh that became mine Help me go through this troubled time Help me to...
Help me to... Help me to...
Look at the bright side
Because you don't know what tomorrow may look like
Tell yourself that sadness is just a lie Made to blind your mind

*Tomorrow will offer you the answer The only truth you deserve
The happiness for which you yearn
Do not be so hard on yourself Those dark days
Will soon be a shadow of themselves
Look now at the bright side Look at your symphony
This little fragile thing we call Baby
A sweet reminder of the role you're playing The Greatest Character: Mother!
You gave birth
This is something you can be proud of Having two hearts instead of just one
So, Look at the bright side
Because tomorrow might take you aback Look at her
Because she is your tomorrow Look at your bright side
Because to her eyes your love will never be a lie
Sometimes all we want is to hibernate inside our mind
Sometimes all we want to see is anything But the Bright side
Look at the bright side Yesterday gave you the answer So, Look at the bright side
Yesterday gave you your tomorrow
Sprinkling your life with smiles & laughter An endless Myriad of falling stars Painting each wall of your mind
With her own colors
Colors of her endless love for her beloved Mother To you
Her laughs will always be worth more than all the world's gold
For you
She will offer her greatest Ode
Bright Side
Help me to spend this new day As another amazing Journey
Help me to transform this adventure with my baby Into great dreams full of happy memories*

Bright side… Bright side…
Bright side, Bright side, here you are! All this time I was holding you in my arms

CAN YOU…
Can you imagine a perfect sanctuary? Devoid of any boundary An ideal receptacle Total abstraction Empty of any restriction
Can you imagine the voices in your mind? Getting their freedom
Speaking on your behalf Transforming each of your frustrations Into something beyond imagination
Can you picture a 'mythical reality'? Granting an endless well of wishes To your latent creativity
A new countdown
A nine-month big bang
Sheltered inside an exponential dome While you are witnessing
A new planet's dawn Gravitating inside your belly Destined, since forever
To be someone else's galaxy
Guiding her to shape her tomorrow
While she is helping you to forget your sorrows Do you realize what you are seeing?
A nine-month dream Named: Between
Interspersing your best past memories With so many others forthcoming

63

Marcia is still brushing May Sissy's hair. There is a long silence that seems to stretch on endlessly for May Sissy, who throws furtive glances at her mother in the mirror, while confronting her own reflection. Her face is soft but expressionless. This non-expression is now painfully reminding her of the abandonment, reveling now to kowtow as would any obedient, submissive girl who swapped her persona and freedom for a silenced pretty little face. The reflection May Sissy now sees is so different from what she used to be. She was solar, expansive, inspired by every beat of her heart. She had a deep and unshakable courage, a little rebellious and a true free spirit. However, sitting before the mirror at this very moment makes her feel hollow. The mirror mirroring this perfect reflection of her current personality, or rather the lack of it. Worse still, as castrating as her mother may be, she has the merit of having retained a personality of her own to which she has remained faithful to this day, never faltering, unlike May Sissy. *Where's the May Sissy that I used to be? What is that look? This gaze doesn't belong to me.* Her eyes are like two chrysalides inside which her stillborn emancipation is forever captured. *That's it! End of the road May! Childhood is over... But what childhood? Can you try to catch up and have a second chance to enjoy something close to the simple pleasures of childhood and the moments of joy that you missed? In your 20s? Maybe... but probably not. Have you seen adults? Adulthood is nothing like childhood!* A word suddenly hits May Sissy's mind: Responsibilities! *Responsibilities?* The inner voice in her mind makes then this naive remark, *Responsibilities Isn't like the equivalent of adulthood certificate or something?* There's nothing worse than looking at yourself and seeing a stranger instead. Feeling the passage of time. May Sissy suddenly feels the weight of the years. The sudden and painful reality knocked her out, handicapping her mind like a stroke for what seemed like a lifetime. She realized then that she had a very short window of time before becoming her mother for good. Her mind is submerged with this sudden swirl of information and revelations. Life can be very short. Life can be unfair. Life can be painful… These new overwhelming epiphanic revelations start causing an inner-dizziness. May Sissy feels like she's shocking. Like an asthma attack. She is out of breath while her brain seems to be boiling. Can you imagine glimpsing into your entire life like supposedly it is when you're about to die? Well, that's what May Sissy experiences for a very brief but traumatizing moment. *What comes after death? Is it total blackness? Everlasting emptiness? And God? Yes! Of course, God wouldn't let that happen! But wait a second! God, do I believe in you?* All these existential questions come rushing, poisoning her mind like a premature middle-life crisis. She is questioning everything. Did she ever believe in God? Or was it formatted? Is she a believer by association? With this mental breakdown, she feels torn apart from inside. Everything seems upside down. Suddenly, she finds it difficult to tell the difference between up and down. It is as though her brain is boiling inside her stomach while her heart is right inside her throat. *'Feel this pressure around your throat? This agony? Well get used to it!'* says the inner voice in her mind. The sudden and brutal understanding of the endless length of Eternity landed as a hard rock in her stomach, sucking out everything in its way, leaving nothing but the feeling of having had her insides brutally ripped apart by the black hole of sudden and early existential crisis.

'Life, death, time, earth, universe, religions… OH SHIT! OH SHIT! SHIIIIT!' the voice inside May Sissy's head says.

'I'm about to lose my mind! That's it. I finally reached it!'

Instinctively, like a last resort — old habits die hard — she immediately starts mentally reciting:

'Our Father, Who art in heaven Hallowed be Thy Name;

Thy kingdom come, Thy will be done, on earth as it is in heaven.

Give us this day our daily bread, and forgive us our trespasses, as we forgive those who trespass against us; and lead us not into temptation, but deliver us from evil. Amen.'

She immediately hates this thought. It makes her feel like she's buying some faith out of fear when she knew deep down that faith comes from true love, not only for God but for your earthly brothers and sisters, the love for everything surrounding you. May Sissy feels that she is sweating profusely, but strangely from inside. It is as though her body as well as her mind decided to shut off from the outside world. May Sissy is right now in Quarantine inside her own hermetic mind. For the first time she wishes she could blindly abandon herself to faith. To be delivered from this evil that was whispering this torturing truth. But faith is now a foreign tongue from which no comfort comes. She is alone amidst the mayhem in her mind. May Sissy looks down, ready to jump into the precipice, contemplating the welcoming well of sweet madness and despair... *Do I jump? Should I? It is strangely so welcoming! Give up everything. Your sanity...*

Finally, May Sissy is brutally brought back to reality, a reality inside which the mayhem falls silent. A stressful, eerie mute chaos.

"Where were you? For a moment you seemed so far away," Marcia asks, slightly concerned.

'Yeah, for a moment,' retorts the inner voice inside May Sissy's mind. *'A moment...'*

64

A moment. An Eternity of self-reflection I just spent
Buried in the depth of my mind for no one to see Is my own Time capsule
Buried in the depth of my brain Is the tomb of my Childhood

May Sissy's mind is still recovering from this inner journey she's been through. Two personalities now coexist inside her mind, the stranger she became and the newly reborn May Sissy. Whilst falling prey to a schizophrenic cannibalistic-like inner turmoil, she tries regaining control and decides what personality to assume.

Finally, the stranger answers Marcia: "Oh! No-nowhere."

She then asks, feigning interest, "So, and you, how was your day, Mother?"

"Oh, you know," says Marcia, still brushing May Sissy's hair. "Same old, same old." Quietly, focusing on her daughter's hair. However, like the calm preceding the storm, the beginning of the latter starts making its appearance, operating through Marcia's passive aggressive tone of voice. So, every single word defining her day is said like a rapid invisible blade. Each pronunciation, a deceptive pain-inflicting gesture. "Calm… Harmonious…" Sounding more like an interrogation.

"Ah-ah!" lets out a taken aback May Sissy. May Sissy is particularly troubled, for although her mother says each word calmly, she brushes her hair in an increasingly aggressive and punitive manner. Each word Marcia says becomes more of a strange little passive aggressive guessing game to which she alone has the secret.

"Without surprise..." Marcia says.

May Sissy moans in pain, "Ouch!"

However, Marcia keeps combing May Sissy, as if nothing is happening and says, "Without... any... surprises... at... all."

This time May Sissy holds back a groan of pain. It's more intense and sudden, causing her to grimace and bite her lip. Marcia is disarmingly calm and keeps staring at May Sissy in an inquisitive manner. Her stare feels like anvils attached to May Sissy's eyelids, weighing down on them, obliging her to look down as she tries her best to evade her mother's prying eyes. The silence filling the room is so noisy. It is like a harassing mute pandemonium bombarding May Sissy's eardrum. May Sissy holds back a groan of pain while Marcia still continues with the same tone of voice, "Without... any... surprising... discovery..."

This time Marcia's harshness pulls out a tuft of hair. It hurts so much that May Sissy can't hold back a sharp cry of pain.

"Mother, you hurt me!" says May Sissy in a feeble voice. "Oh, do I?" says Marcia, faking surprise.

Now it is clear to May Sissy that the evening will not end with a *'Good night, sleep tight!'* accompanying a kiss on her forehead. No, this evening, she is now sure, will end in an atmosphere of profound desolation and solitude.

In the same stoic tone, Marcia says, "Ah, My poor little angel. Your hair is so tangled."

A silence settles in. During which Marcia continues to untangle May Sissy's hair. May Sissy, as for her, expresses anxious concern with her eyes.

"You've grown so fast! That's life. Now, you're a young woman," Marcia says, brushing May Sissy's hair with the same unsettling calmness.

There's another brief moment of silence before Marcia asks, falsely concerned, "And your menstrual periods? Not too painful?"

"N-No. Wh-Why are you asking?" responds a disconcerted May Sissy, fearing her mother's answer.

Marcia stops brushing her daughter's hair and says, "Oh! Isn't it what a normal mother does? Worrying about her own daughter?"

The same noisy silence remains after Marcia's remark. The mute mayhem spreads at an alarming rate inside May Sissy's mind, like a tentacular virus. Palpitations start to harass May Sissy's heart. May Sissy tries her best not to give in to the growing pressure. But unfortunately, it's a task that's getting harder and harder. Each door inside May Sissy's mind opens to a dead end. Cornered, May Sissy is quickly brought back to reality, as though she were rejected, kicked out of her own mind.

"Isn't it?" Marcia says, insisting.

"Y-Y-Yes. Of course, Mother."

The unspeakable threat looming over the room since Marcia appeared begins to materialize dangerously through the increasingly worrying attitude of Marcia who is now making her, so far deliberately vague, intentions known.

Marcia puts the hairbrush on the bed and immediately opens the drawer of the nightstand on which the new Bible now rests. She reaches for May Sissy's diary; she grabs it and she asks in that same calm tone as she's rising from the edge of the bed, "Well, maybe you can explain to me this then?"

Marcia's piercing eyes and serious look are suddenly like the brutal blow of a sharp knife to May Sissy's stomach. May Sissy is petrified. For a very brief moment it's like she's having an inner seizure.

Marcia opens May Sissy's diary to a particular page that she begins to read aloud, "April 16, 1968.

Dear Diary,

Today makes it a year since I had my menarche. I have had my first kiss with a boy named Martial. He is black, and I believe he is a little older than me. Maybe two years. I'm not really sure. He loves animals like me and wants to become a veterinarian or an animal rights activist.

I realize that what grandfather says about them is completely wrong. They are educated people much more interesting than many of the so-called civilized white Americans."

Marcia turns some pages from the diary and continues reading, "July 25, 1969.

Dear Diary,

I feel and continue to feel a growing physical desire, but I do not know if I really should give in to the temptation. Mother claims that the shameless as she calls them who offer themselves to the pleasures of the flesh before marriage will all go straight to hell. I'm a little afraid of the intercourse, for it appears to be painful, at least the first time, and what if my period starts during intercourse?"

As she stops reading, Marcia gives May Sissy a stern look. May Sissy seems horrified. One can easily have guessed that now the worst she expected would be welcome compared to what she is experiencing this very moment. It sure looks like a one-way ticket to desolation-land.

Marcia then repeats a passage of her daughter's personal diary, as May Sissy stares at her in total dismay.

"I feel and continue to feel a growing physical desire…"

Marcia then grabs a book from the drawer and says with the most profound disdain as she's holding it, "And 'that'! *Carrie*. A novel of a girl possessed with a terrifying power." She then adds with the same contempt, "I see."

Marcia turns the book over and begins to read the synopsis:

Carrie White, seventeen years old, lonely, shy and not very pretty, lives a nightmare: she is the victim of her mother's religious fanaticism and… She abruptly interrupts her reading and says, "No need to read more. I've already read enough."

Her aversion grows as she thumbs through the book.

"Stephen King, huh! Another one of those fools, who have nothing better to do than writing that kind of nonsense they call a story!"

"But I like his book!" says May Sissy as she's rising awkwardly from her chair. Marcia replies in a sententious tone,

"Well, maybe you'll end up just like him: burning in hell for all eternity."

Hearing these cruel words, May Sissy seems even more fragile than ever and she bursts into tears of despair and sadness as she says, "Don't say that!"

Because even though her faith has somewhat diminished over the years (preferring books such as Carrie over the Bible; the two not being obligatorily incompatible and should be allowed to coexist inside May Sissy's mind instead of being perceived as angel and devil sitting upon her shoulders), hearing her own mother wishing her to go to hell gives her a dreadful sense of haunting hopelessness.

Marcia looks again through her daughter's diary. She opens it again to July 25, 1969 and reluctantly begins to read it, for the second time, submerged in her aversion. This time, only her lips are moving but no sound comes out of her mouth. She reads it to herself. It appears that Marcia wants to make sure. Sure, that the text, the ink, the paper is real. Knowing herself, for a very brief moment, the loving mother in her kicks in and for a very precious moment, she wishes she didn't find anything else besides her daughter's new Bible. No. The loving mother in her wishes she hadn't felt the urge to pry. These precious brief moments are Legion. But unfortunately, what can a Legion of dead stars do but shine from very far away, from the utmost extremity of Marcia soul.

Marcia stops reading and turns her attention to her daughter, while repeating a specific short passage of the diary that seems to wind her up, "During intercourse? During intercourse!" expecting her daughter to deny what's written in the diary.

Her eyes more pervasive than ever now seem to try to read through a petrified May Sissy. There is a long and dreadful anticipation filled silence. Marcia grows impatient by the second but fights to keep control of herself while her eyes seem to be this perfectly balanced contradiction.

Marcia then starts showing signs of impatience, glaring furiously at May Sissy while demanding emphatically, "Well, then?"

"No! We didn't do it," protests May Sissy, trying to appear insulted by her mother's accusations but coming off even more frail, powerless.

"And how can I be sure?"

"Don't you think that if we had really done it, that I would have been pregnant by now?" With these words Marcia strikes a violent slap across May Sissy's sweet face. The harshness of the slap is slightly tempered as May Sissy moves backward in her chair. May Sissy realizes that the discharge of the slap really owes its powerful and meaningful effect to — thanks to her own narrow-minded, mainly fanatism-themed thesaurus — the electrically conductive properties of the harshness of Marcia's words.

"If indeed you had gotten pregnant, particularly from him, you wouldn't be in this house in this very moment! But, since that does not prove anything, there is only one way to be sure," says Marcia, filled with suppressed anger.

"Please! Please, Mother! Don't make me do this! Please! Do not force me to do that!" implores May Sissy. May Sissy's face is covered in a sea of tears, while she's overcome by this spreading, crippling complete bleakness.

"Come on! You don't leave me much choice. So, come on now. Raise your dress."

During these moments of power trip, a new piece of Marcia's soul was breaking in several other little pieces. Marcia knew that. She was like a spectator of her own actions. Unable to stop. May Sissy now misses the feeling of being safe. It's almost like Marcia, being in this case the metaphorical amniotic fluid, doesn't want to let go of May Sissy while May Sissy on the other hand is longing to birth. While Marcia keeps mentally convincing herself *'I just want to keep you away from the belly of the beast this world can be. A child should never have to leave the mother womb if this is the kind of world that welcomes it.'*

Love can be blind. May Sissy feels guilty for not

understanding her mother, for not being able to put herself in her shoes, or rather for putting herself in her shoes but still realizing that their points of view differ. She knows her mother's love is the sincerest feeling in the world but... the way she sees it, or rather the way she pictures it in an oversimplified childish way, is:

Religious Marcia = lie detector Loving mother = Amniotic fluid

May Sissy tasted her very first glass of wine last Thanksgiving and right now she is reminiscing of the feelings that invaded her body and mind, so warm and relaxing. Strangely, at this moment, she only saw the best of her mother. She felt optimistic and safe. She addictively welcomed her own submissive nature with open arms. She stared at her mother's eyes and felt cocooned inside the warmest and safest place in the whole world.

She now knows that the fanatic Marcia was the equivalent of the hangover that generally follows these ephemeral moments. She remembers everything going in a surreal slow motion. The memory is even more painful, as it is a testament of how much time May Sissy spent with the hangover and how special but rare and brief were the sweet moments spent with Marcia the loving mother. No kid should have to long for her mother when the mother was there all along...

Maybe for Mother the outside world is like when people are wasted, or like the hangover that inevitably follows. It is noisy, giving you the headache.

A double-edged distorted mirror. May Sissy remembers how the liquid that goes through your system makes you feel like you're back to the safety of your mother's amniotic fluid. An endless universe devoid of any knowledge and consequences, just this forgotten 9-month blessed feeling. May Sissy heard about depression but until now never really understood the true meaning of it. She just thought it was an illness that could be cured with some medication. She now understands the powerful grip of this cancer of the mind. She now gets that there's more than one way to go in life. *Can you be tired of life? Can sadness and deep despair actually kill you?* It's funny how innocent and naive you can be when you're a kid! Full of life, passion, curiosity. Everything is new, everything is amazing, grandiose, and most of all everything is everlasting…

DISTORTING MIRROR
Out of character Out of reach Out of touch Out of the blue
Walking away from any smile
Wondering how to write the perfect Ode to you
I'm in the attic of my mind
Feels like I've been living there since the dawn of time
I can't scream any more
I gave up my vocal cords
I'm now on the highway I'm almost at the border Trying to flee far away From this Distorting Mirror

Anywhere But There!
ONE DAY LATER

"Anywhere but there! Anywhere but there!"

She is now a reborn May Sissy, who has finally transcended her fear, her suffering, and who runs for the very first time out of her breathless life, running like crazy through the ocean of fir trees. The day before had apparently been the trigger, the eagerly awaited click, the one that drove the slumbering courage deep within her for an eternity to rise. This is now a May Sissy who has her thirst for freedom back. The more she puts some distance between her and Rocky Tank Town, the more she runs out of steam, the more she feels alive, every breath being imbued with a rage of freedom. May Sissy runs for her survival. For her sanity. Every breath and every step seem like a victory in her eyes, as she repeats frantically to herself this short Mantra-like motivational phrase,

"Anywhere but there! Anywhere but there! Anywhere but there! Anywhere but there!"

She's wearing a long khaki coat wide open and a denim overall dress with her ballet flats. She runs without once looking behind her. Her long cascade of hair loose dancing freely. Frantically penduluming from one side to the other. Her wide leather shoulder bag around her shoulder. The deeper she gets into the forest, the more her lungs fill up with a whiff of freedom. While continuing to run, tears begin to appear in her eyes. The big difference is that this time it's tears of joy, of liberation.

May Sissy slows down and eventually stops to catch her breath. And as she's panting, she bursts out in a few minor bouts of laughter. While she catches her breath, she looks up at the sky. The night seems to be falling for a long time already, revealing a beautiful starry sky somewhat obstructed by the horde of majestic firs competing in beauty, while hooting owls resound like a peaceful and comforting lullaby. May Sissy stands motionless, head up, eyes closed, enjoying the perfection that surrounds her, enjoying this perfect, balanced harmony. Inspirational moment of meditation strengthening her senses. She stands there for a long time.

Upon opening her eyes, May Sissy looks furtively over her shoulder, but all she managed to see, to her great relief, is this same stretch of fir trees as far as the eye can see. She appears to have apparently managed to put enough distance between her and Rocky Tank Town. However, she still continues her course and returns to running through the forest. May Sissy runs for a while without looking back. Her free long hair, her long open coat and her wide leather shoulder bag are dancing again. The dark depths in front of her seem to show her the way to go: straight ahead without looking back, without hesitation. Running again and again. Running toward her emancipation. Running toward her (re)birth. Even the cries of hooting owls come to her ears as cries of encouragement for her to accelerate the pace. Her eyes lit with a sudden fervor to live.

May Sissy then hears distant sounds, the sudden roar of what appears to be a very large bear. His roar is like a horrible, haunting cry of agony. While continuing to run, May Sissy tries to hide. However, when she turns her head again, May Sissy is suddenly hit in the face, plunging her into instant darkness.

68

NOVEMBER 22, 2012
Martial, leaning back against the sink, wipes his glass using the towel he holds in his hand and says in his usual caustic

tone, only more bitter, "Yeah, that's right. I almost forgot God's strange sense of humor."

Martial rubs his forehead with his hands, slightly upset. Since his son's untimely departure — found beaten to death in the alley behind a bar, after having naively expressed some reservations about the Iraq war, pointing out similarities between the invasion of Iraq and the invasion of Poland, comparing 9/11 to 1933 Reichstag fire, and the speech of the US Secretary of State Colin Powell to the defensive war of 1939 in Poland —, whenever he felt a conversation swerved too close to everything key to God's will, Martial felt irritated, which was usually followed by an intense migraine, as it is the case in this very moment.

As Martial is about to abruptly leave the kitchen, Mindy asks him with a surprised look, while continuing to peel the green beans in the bowl, "Where are you going now?"

"Just going for a walk," says Martial, leaving the kitchen. The tone of his voice doesn't invite her to ask more questions, Mindy seems to understand that. She understands that her son needs time for himself and respects it without questioning him further.

69

Polina — still wearing her very thick coat and chic white fur — stands in front of the church. Her eyes are fixated on the big, imposing ten and a half feet long stuffed brown bear in the middle of the roundabout. She has a somewhat morbid curiosity.

Although the rain has finally stopped falling, the gray clouds have remained in position seemingly even more capricious, a looming threat of gray shadows, such as a water leak repaired by an amateur and preparing to burst open at any moment.

And while all the businesses, as well as the library and school, are closed and complete silence reigns, while Polina seems lost far across the stuffed brown bear, Martial, wearing his coat, passes silently by the church, stopping near Polina, and taking some time before noticing her presence. Polina sees Martial standing a little further and smoking a cigarette. She takes the opportunity to start a conversation by saying 'hi' in a friendly tone with a warm smile, "Hey! I'm sorry, by the way. I was a bit rude and impolite…"

Realizing her poor choice of word, she immediately adds in a muttered voice, more to herself, "Which are the exact same things."

Polina has this tendency to approach anyone with this disconcerting assurance, regardless of whether the person is of her age group or Martial's.

"I guess it's this place that makes me feel nervous."

"That's okay. No need to apologize. I know what you mean. I used to live here, but I always felt like a stranger in this place," Martial says calmly, puffing on his cigarette.

There is a lengthy silence during which Martial stares at the stuffed brown bear with a wry look, puffing on his cigarette.

Polina looks a little expressionless and then says, "We were meant to meet, me and that hole. We both belong to the night."

Martial briefly looks amused, and Polina also smiles briefly. They both enjoy this trivial but gratifying moment of sharing.

Then Martial looks away, smoking his cigarette, as once again a lengthy silence settles between them.

Polina breaks the new silence after about a minute, "Everything is so creepy here." Immediately adding, "Especially the damn witch at the drug store."

Looking distracted, Martial says, "She wasn't always like that."

Polina looks furtively at her watch and says, "I better go home."

Martial says nothing. He just nods at her briefly. Polina is getting ready to walk toward R.A. Minnesota Avenue located on the right but stops and says to Martial, "Oh, by the way!"

"Huh?"

"Have a nice Thanksgiving!"

"Thanks, you too," Martial answers politely.

Martial hates the shell of bitterness and lassitude he has become. This dark, serious, laconic character.

Polina turns and walks down the still wet and glistening avenue of R.A. Minnesota Avenue.

Martial halts for a moment in front of the church before which he now seems so ridiculously insignificant. This church, still unchanged with its imposing, dark and gleaming stature stands as this guardian of the perfect equilibrium between order and morality.

Martial looks upwards at the top of the church and the morose sky.

70

Polina seems to have lost a little of her self-confidence, as she's walking on R.A. Minnesota Avenue. The ground is as black as coal and in the same poor condition as in the past, completely cratered in some places. R.A. Minnesota Avenue still appears to have been hit by a shower of mini meteorites. Just like the ground, the homes haven't changed much either. On the contrary, the years have not played out in their favor, as it could be the case for some buildings, which sometimes have a rustic look. Here, everything seems to be in a state of neglect and disrepair. There is a sense of abandonment, which gives the street a ghostly appearance. Even the absolute quietude prevailing there does not seem natural.

This eerie scenery puts Polina in an anxious state as she walks cautiously down the street and says to herself, "Really creepy… damn! Now I sound like Owen Wilson! Reeeaally creepy!"

She finally comes to the end of the R. A. Minnesota Avenue, leading to the junction between Grand Street, on the right, R. A. Minnesota Avenue on the left, and on the opposite side Rusty Street, toward which Polina walks immediately.

Polina arrives at her parents' residence. Their MPV is still parked outside in the same place. As she's about to enter the house, Polina realizes that the drug store is about to close when she sees the metallic gray blinds being lowered. She remains motionless for a moment, staring at the drug store. After a moment of reflection, she says aloud enough, with a newfound insolence, "Have a nice Thanksgiving too, Creepy bitch."

She then moves toward the low wire fence in front of the house. Its fifteen square feet is being used as a garden, a poor and desolate garden in which only wild grass grows. She walks through the narrow-paved driveway, that ends fifteen feet ahead at four marble steps, which lead to the house. At first glance, the house seems to be a pretty good investment apart from some slightly flaking pink paint. It has solid foundations, and it is fairly spacious. As Polina crosses the driveway, she looks at it with disdain. The gray sky hovers over the house. Its dark veil inspiring nothing but gloom. As she heads for the four front steps, she turns her head slightly toward Rusty Street. She scans it with a contemptuous look. Then she continues climbing the steps. Reaching the front door of the house, Polina digs a hand into her pocket and pulls out a key. She opens the door and enters the house. She closes the front door behind her, disappearing inside.

As she enters the hall, Polina takes a good look at the inside of the house. She looks puzzled. At first glance, the rooms seem to be arranged the same way as Marcia's, the only difference being that instead of the usual furniture, carpets and other household items, the hall and the corridor are filled with untouched boxes. Polina is quite surprised to see that the boxes are still where they were before she went out early in the morning. "Hey!"

She's waiting for an answer from her mother and/or father, but the only response she gets is this almost oppressive silence reigning in the house.

"Hello? C'mon, guys!"

The floor of the entrance corridor is made of lavish and impeccable shiny brown parquet. On the left is a nine feet high wall with a staircase leading up to the second floor. The walls are covered with new beige wallpaper.

After another equally heavy silence that seems to last forever, Polina says with weariness, "Whatever."

As she turns her head to the right toward the living room, Polina's suddenly hit in the head by someone or something she does not have the time to identify and immediately falls into unconsciousness.

71

May Sissy is coming around very slowly. The blackout lasted about ten minutes. She slowly opens an eye, followed by the other, while the plaintive roars of the bear now seem to be very nearby. Her vision is still unclear, blinded by a thick veil, while her hearing seems to play tricks on her, harassing her still comatose mind with noises coming to her brutally like electroshocks. For the moment, she's barely able to distinguish her own hands in front of her. All she notices is the blood that seems to cover them. All she knows at the moment is that she is down against a tree and bleeding somewhere, and given the incessant migraine, the blood on her hands probably came from her head. As she turns her head frantically around, panicked, breathing heavily, all she manages to perceive is still the same blurred vision while the roars of agony from the bear sound so close to her. While she's there, unable to fully trust her sight and hearing, May Sissy is totally powerless. In a flurry of panic, words force their way between her lips, "W-What! W-Who? Oh, P-Please!" she stammers, frantically turning her head, as she hears the roars of the bear all around her. The bear's roars are accompanied by a noise that sounds as if the animal is crawling on the ground. There is the sound of claws scraping metal immediately followed by a new roar. This time much more haunting and yet heartbreaking, for it sounds like the distressful roar of a dying beast.

"Aah!" shouts a panic-stricken May Sissy, expecting the bear to pounce on her at any moment.

Gradually her vision improves, each element slowly becoming clearer. Now she can clearly see both of her hands in front of her, covered in blood. Instinctively, May Sissy passes her hand over her face and realizes that the blood must come from the top of her forehead, because she feels a sudden and sharp pain when she touches it.

May Sissy is lost and frightened in the middle of the forest.

Her eyes suddenly catch something that she did not expect, something whose presence frightens her. A very large brown bear measuring at least ten and a half feet long just two feet away from her. He lies slouched miserably on his stomach; one of its front legs weakly moves up and then almost immediately falls down in front of him. He is just two feet away from the petrified May Sissy. Not a sound coming out of her mouth. The bear's eyes and May Sissy's eyes meet. His eyes are those of a dying frightened soul approaching Quietus doors. It is possible that the bear is more afraid than May Sissy at this moment. However, she knows what it feels like to be afraid and abandoned, she sees the dejected look in the eyes of the brown bear, a look that May Sissy knows only too well. The bear tries again to roar, but now with so little strength, the only thing that manages to come out of his mouth is a low moan. Trying to overcome her fear, May Sissy leans over slightly and realizes that one of the two rear legs of the brown bear is caught in a massive bear trap. At that moment the only sounds are the hoots from the owls, the occasional sound of leaves in the wind and the uneven breathing and rumbling of a dying brown bear. May Sissy's face is stained with blood from a large cut on her forehead. She hesitates a moment, looking at the dying bear with sympathy. Like a quirk of fate. They were like spectators — sitting on the passenger seat — of their own existence. Their two stories colliding. Two sacrificial beings, rejected upon the altar of a universal neutral chaos and impartial bleakness.

May Sissy tries to recover, and sits awkwardly on one knee, however, she soon realizes that she has not yet fully recovered all of her reflexes and starts to wobble dangerously.

She barely avoids falling down by grabbing on to the tree against which she had been lying a moment ago.

Resting against the tree, May Sissy has difficulty getting up, and after kneeling on the ground for a while, she finally manages to recover completely on her two legs. But she has barely straightened up, when she hears a voice shouting, "She's over there, Dad! I see her!"

This voice isn't unknown to May Sissy. The voice is Coby Swinton's voice, who had always been, in May Sissy's eyes, a pretentious asshole like his barbarian father. Both were hunters. If there had been a license to hunt humans, Mr. Swinton would probably have been the first to get it. They would hunt anything and everything without any qualms. Then they would go to church on Sunday to wash away all of their sins and ease their conscience the rest of the week. Being close friends of May Sissy's mother, they had to be immediately aware of her absence and join the search party... much to May Sissy's dismay.

A little further — about ninety feet away — nineteen-year-old Coby appears holding a rifle in his hands and running toward May Sissy. As he gets closer, his father appears too. He's about fifty years old, with a weathered face. He too is holding a rifle in his hands.

Finally, arriving at about thirty feet away, they both become aware of the presence of the brown bear, harmless and dying on the ground.

Without taking a second to assess the situation, Coby's father says as he immediately points his gun at the poor animal, "Be careful Coby! Over there!"

At this point, everything is accelerating. A shot is fired and hits the back leg of the bear already caught in the trap. The bear cries out in agony. The heartbreaking cries reach the ears of Coby and his father, who surely perceives this as a threat, because soon after the first bullet hit the bear's back leg, a second bullet leaves the barrel of Coby's rifle. This time the bullet hits the hip of the brown bear which again lets out a haunting roar. The bullet hardly reaches the bear's hip than Coby already fires at the defenseless, agonizing bear's paw, barely two feet from May Sissy, who is more terrified by Coby and his father than by the harmless brown bear lying on the ground.

Coby aims his gun at the front leg of the bear and once more pulls the trigger while May Sissy screams, "NO! DON'T!"

But it is already too late. The fourth bullet comes right through the front leg of the brown bear, splashing blood everywhere. Under the horrified gaze of May Sissy, trapped, overwhelmed by a sudden sensation of disillusionment… And guilt by association. Coby and his father arrive in front of the brown bear and May Sissy. They shoot two additional shots almost point blank at the animal. The fifth bullet hits the bear in the neck and the sixth and final one lodges itself in the head, killing the beast once and for all.

Smoke escapes from the bullet holes on the bear's head and neck, while May Sissy looks almost catatonic, with a haunting expression of abandonment and stupor upon her traumatized face.

At that moment, there is complete silence, as though the forest is mourning the death of the brown bear in its own way.

CHAPTER TWO
GROUNDSWELL

1

Polina is slowly emerging from her blackout. She hears many different sounds like stifled groans, and cutlery being set on a table. Polina hears the fuzzy sounds reaching her from a distance. Sounds interfered with by a loud crackling resulting from the blow she received to the head. The muffled groan reaches her ears again. They are becoming increasingly distinct, sounding like those of a gagged person trying to scream.

After some time, Polina gets her hearing back.

She first opens one eye. Everything is blurred around her. Then she opens the other. Yet all is still blurry. Her hearing takes as much time to return as her sight. She needs to get used to the sudden light from a place she is still unable to identify. She doesn't know where she is. All she perceives are vague images like flashes assaulting her weakened eyes. A new stifled groan, more intense this time, rings in Polina's right ear. She immediately turns her head and catches a glimpse of something that resembles the silhouette of someone sitting on a chair and struggling vigorously. The person groans again this time desperately as if it was the last groan they'll ever make. Panic washes over Polina as she struggles to say something, interrupted by her sudden jerky breathing, "Ah! A-A-Ah, ah!

Wh-Wh-Wh... What is...?"

A mystery voice addresses her suddenly, a soft voice, teasing Polina whose sight is still feeble:

"Over here, Honey!"

Polina turns her head around frantically, trying to find whoever is talking to her while she tries once again to articulate words, "Wh-Wh-Wh... What is... Who is...?"

Polina distinguishes the silhouette of a woman standing up by the other end of a long table. The woman then says in the same soft and engaging voice, still playing — sadistically messing — with Polina, "There you go! Over here, Honey!"

Now that Polina's eyesight is slowly returning to normal, she discovers, horrified, panic-stricken, that she is strapped with barbed wire coiled around her bruised and bloodied wrists and ankles fastened on the armrests and legs of an old wooden chair. On her right, is her mother, wearing the same clothes as before, tied up the same way and gagged with a piece of old fabric. She tries to speak to her daughter, but all that comes out of her mouth is a stifled groan. Julianne seems a bit reassured to see Polina regain consciousness, although she wishes she hadn't come home. But there they are, powerless, bound together for some reason unknown to them. Even if there was a reason, would it justify this?

"Mom! Mom! What happened? W-Where's Dad?" cries a terrified Polina while looking at her mother with eyes of terror and confusion.

Questions her mother answers with groans.

Polina looks up and sees May Sissy, who is standing before her on the other side of a large table, covered with a white lace tablecloth on which is set a feast in the purest Thanksgiving tradition. In the center, there is a large white soup tureen containing pumpkin soup with a ladle, mashed sweet potatoes, cranberry jelly, buttered bread, green bean casserole, apple pie and a pecan pie, pumpkin cake and wine. However, there is no stuffed turkey on the table. In fact, there is no meat at all on the table. Aside from the table and the living room, it is completely empty, devoid of furniture, illuminated by an ordinary white ceiling lamp for just the middle of the room above the table.

May Sissy appears to have developed some kind of Stockholm syndrome. She stands before this feast, wearing a long and beautiful navy-blue velvet dress with a white collar with her hair tied in a low bun, just like her mother, Marcia, used to. May Sissy holds a large cutting knife whose blade is covered with blood. The knife blade is stuck in the wooden table.

May Sissy, whose eyes are now lit with some madness — like those of an unhinged schizophrenic — then says, "Oh, well, well, well! At last, the insomniac wakes up!"

Polina's face is smeared with blood that oozes from a wound on her forehead. Some of her hair is mingled with the blood.

"Wh-What do you want from us? Why are you doing this? A-And w-w-where's my father?" stammers Polina on the verge of tears.

She then cracks and scream apoplectically "W-W-WHAT THE FUCK!"

May Sissy suddenly loses patience. She has this profound frustrated expression on her face. She removes the big knife covered in blood from the table. It makes a sudden threatening noise as the blade cuts through the wood, ejecting tiny wood chips.

She then says with a mad look, "What the fuck? I'm

gonna tell you what the fuck! It's this world that's fucked up!"

May Sissy looks so serious now. She stares at the knife she's holding, temporarily forgetting Polina and her mother. Despite the horror of her act, a certain degree of humanity appears on her face, almost touching. She's got the tortured look of a bruised soul trapped inside a shallow shell whose loneliness has attracted madness, corrupting her personality into this bitter, vengeful presence only driven by unfinished business, standing now in this macabre scene.

Whilst May Sissy stares silently at the bloody blade that she holds in her hand, Polina — whose wrists are cut deeply by the barbed wires, forcing grunts of pain from her, while drops of blood begin to flow along the chair she sits on — cracks under the weight of the pain and panic overcoming her and cries out, furious and panicked, "THEN WHAT DO YOU WANT FROM US YOU FUCKING LUNATIC!"

May Sissy starts to walk toward Polina in a very slow and serene way, while dragging the blade of the knife along the table. Polina and her mother, powerless, are looking at the blade, impedingly approaching them.

May Sissy reaches Polina who is now embedded in a puddle of tears, tears of panic and, tears of despair. She is realizing that her short life is probably about to be prematurely and brutally abbreviated. The thought of this terrifies her, to the point of peeing herself while shaking nervously, convulsively. The warm liquid wet her crotch and starts smearing along her legs.

May Sissy starts to wave the blade of her knife at Polina's face as she says in an ominously serene voice, "Can you feel this despair? This despair that makes you realize that your short life is probably about to be prematurely and brutally abbreviated."

Then while she is behind Polina, disappearing from her sight, she starts to very slowly slide this knife shaped impending doom along the back of the chair, accentuating Polina's frantic state of panic. As she turns her head frantically, she looks at her mother, who tries to wave at her, while letting out a deep muffled groan. Her eyes bulge with fear.

At this moment, May Sissy's calm voice reaches Polina's ears, "Isn't that what does your father for a living after all? Isn't that what he does to beautify your life? Shorten prematurely and brutally the lives of animals?" She now stands facing Polina and adds, "And all of this for what, huh? So that you can proudly strut around wearing that shit!" She slowly brushes the blade of the knife against Polina's fur coat.

"Aah! P-Please! W-W-Wait!" staggers Polina. And then she blindly takes her chance with the desperate lie '*de la dernière chance*', the kind of obvious lie that anyone could come up with in a situation where reason has abandoned one's mind.

"B-But I'm a v-v-vegetarian like you, you know!" Obvious lie to which May Sissy says, faking puzzlement, "Oh, really?"

"Yeah! I swear to God! I am!" says Polina desperately. Her tearful eyes are suddenly lit with a desperate ounce of hope.

May Sissy sarcastically retorts, "But you said, and I quote, 'It's not my fault if I like them on my plate!' Oh yes and I forgot the charming 'Creepy bitch' at the end. But don't worry I won't be mad at you for that little hint of affection. I have inherited this quality from my mother." She pauses and then adds, "You thought because I live here, that I don't have TV or internet? Is that what you thought?"

Giving in under the weight of panic and not really wanting

to upset a woman who's pointing a huge knife in her face, Polina says in tears, "No! It's not what I think about you, of course not!"

Grimacing nervously, May Sissy says, "No. Of course you don't."

"Please! Please! Don't... Don't... Don't kill me!" Polina cries powerlessly while blood flows from her wrists. She's as powerless as a lamb in a slaughterhouse. It is terrifying to come to the realization that your fate lies in the hands of an unbalanced character. Strange things go through our minds during extremely stressful moments. It is almost like your brain is shielding itself from overdosing. Right now, Polina prays to God not to be found soiled with piss and shit. Even facing death, we desperately try to conserve some dignity.

Unfortunately, she's brutally brought back to reality, as May Sissy says, "Oh, no! We haven't even tasted the turkey yet. What kind of host would I be, if I killed you before the turkey?"

"B-B-But you-y-you said you were a vegetarian?" staggers Polina.

May Sissy then pours herself a glass of wine while speaking to Polina, "Yes, indeed. You just asked me where your father is. I think it's time I should confess that I haven't had enough time to buy a turkey."

"W-W-What does that mean? W-W-W-Where's my father?" asks Polina, fearing the answer she already knows.

"Don't worry. He should be joining us soon." May Sissy says very calmly with an unsettlingly haunting serene saw-blade grin.

2

"Why should they ask me to put on a uniform and go 10,000 miles away from home and drop bombs and bullets on Brown people in Vietnam while so-called Negro people in Louisville are treated like dogs and denied simple human rights? No, I'm not going 10,000 miles away from home to help murder and burn another poor nation simply to continue the domination by white slave masters of darker people the world over.

"This is the day when such evils must come to an end. I have been warned that to take such a stand would cost me millions of dollars. But I have said it once and I will say it again. The real enemy of my people is here. I will not disgrace my religion, my people or myself by becoming a tool to enslave those who are fighting for their own justice, freedom and equality. If I thought the war was going to bring freedom and equality to 22 million of my people they wouldn't have to draft me, I'd join tomorrow. I have nothing to lose by standing up for my beliefs. So, I'll go to jail, so what? We've been in jail for 400 years."

— MUHAMMAD ALI —

3

SAUTON

Poetic anthology Written by Lawrence Tyrese Sillons

'*DYSTOPIAN UTOPIA*'
I've seen tomorrow's first fruit Why did it look like yesterday's consequences? A forgotten past's reminiscences
Sunset, sunset, sunset
Brother, welcoming the twilight Twilight, twilight, twilight

Sister, welcoming the night...
So tired, so, so tired...
Why am I bleeding tears? While I see this world?
Vision of horror Past of murders Present a lot worse
And a future already sold to the highest bidder
Why do these red drops fall upon my face?
And why do they have this damn bloody taste?
Our worst enemy is the one who sleeps inside every one of us
Capable of the best but also mostly of the worst
Since the very beginning Man has wanted everything
Century after century, need became a whim And whims became our sins
Massacres and crimes became skills, Torture became a second nature
Lands of blood won by a bunch of greedy fools
Guns and nuclear bombs have become tools Hands full of shiny gold
Making man believe he's some kind a god
Leaving Oceans and earths full of blood and shame While flows in my veins
From my brain
My blood Color: Memories
Of a better world for posterity!
I'm the man lost in his own lyrics
Wondering what legacy do we want to leave behind
An eye for an Eye Rhyme for Rhyme A tooth for a tooth
Now is the time of Truth Decide or choose
Where's the difference? After all, in the end
All is left is the consequences I'm the man lost in his own lyrics
Wondering what legacy, we want to leave behind Has the world become completely mad?

All I know is I don't want to be part of your perpetual cockfight!
While all I'm crying is that Ink
With which I wrote this Scathing attack!
Why are our eyes crying dust?
Why doesn't our heart beat any more? Maybe because we're cursed
Maybe for having sold our soul Or maybe for having built empires All over the globe
We can continue to hide behind our own lies But the real matter is
What legacy do we want to leave behind? Sooner or later, to them
We'll owe apologies
Cause, the only ones to blame will be ourselves For having left to the future owners
A world full of blood and graves Corpses, dust and shame Be free to live or die
But don't expect someone will help you to survive
That's why I've broke the rules Cause, I didn't want to play your role
I am the scourge of the so-called moral Dictated by some morons
Sent to break the rusted chains of hypocrisy To leave at least something behind me
Something for my legacy
I'm the man lost in his own lyrics
Wondering what legacy do we want to leave behind
An eye for an Eye Rhyme for Rhyme A tooth for a tooth
Now is the time of Truth
Decide or choose Where's the difference? After all, in the end

All that is left is the consequences
Has the world become completely mad? All I know is that I don't want to be part of your perpetual cockfight!
And, against the odds, Here I am spitting this Ode!
Into the existential crisis of some individuals Chaos
Sees a potential new host
A fraud, self-proclaimed Hope
Preaching that 'Peace is from now on a taboo subject' False Dogma
Keeping its subjects
Away from what it most dreads An iron fist in a velvet glove
Reigning all over the Globe Dictatorial democracy
Ruling this dysfunctional society Peace is pissed off!
Paranoia told her to get lost Freedom is no longer welcome
Something beautiful is about to occur I'm starting to hear the whisper of what seems to be a glimmer of lassitude of this servitude!
Did mankind become synonym of genocide? Is it too late? Or is it still time?
History is filled with mistakes But also full of acts of bravery
So maybe we can change and put behind us all these atrocities
So, let's see...

VOLATILE!
Intro: **Ego-System**
When people cannot bear their reality And look at the bright side
They look at the last light They seek... suicide...
Instead of going against the tide
I wish... I wish...
I wish...

There wouldn't have been so many genocides in so little time...
I had a disturbing dream last night I was sitting before a skeleton Then, I realized
That, Me it was
Another ghost who into this huge Ego-System has been trapped
Another fish who by these Jellyfishes has been marked
Everything around us falls apart
But why do they seem to be the only ones not to be taken aback?
Admiring the sad spectacle unfolding as their masterpiece
While everything around us falls in pieces...
Is that sweat or tears? No! This is blood!
It's red. The color of guiltiness
And it is your culpability that is gushing No! They're not blushing! They're bleeding!
Crying drops of despair and wearing a red coat of sadness
And, this is on your hands!
Your responsibility begins from the very moment you open your mouth
So, please, do us a favor... SHUT THE HELL UP!
Can't you see they want this masquerade to end!
I swear to say the truth, The whole truth
And nothing but the truth So help me God
Mine happens to be unapologetic
Deal with it!
They raped our self-confidence Optimizing their chance to obtain from us a total obedience
Conditioning our mind
Till we finally blindly believe
That reality is a fatality that we cannot fight Assuring us that

*the strange symptoms we're experiencing are regressing
Leaving us with a Stockholm syndrome Increasing
Overwhelmed by the stench of their gibberish Keeping you on leash
The so-called policing That polices everyone
Making damn sure you're keeping a low profile Muzzling your mind
By putting it under guardianship With their Mumbo-Jumbo
Putting your free will under embargo
They shape their own truth Making of lies the only proof
Subliminal messages sent by these misfortune tellers
Creating tomorrow's genocidal messengers
They think their shadow is big enough to hide their crimes
They think their speech sounds smart
But lies have the same taste in any language And will always smell like garbage
They swallowed the key of this perpetual captivity Freedom is nowadays a reward
While soldiers say 'Au-revoir' To their family
Drained of all personality
Killing each other for that ounce of liberty They're shooting with guns loaded with hypocrisy Disguising their compulsive need for supremacy As a so-called insecurity
Making them believe they're brave When all they see it's a bunch of slaves This is insane!
Modern Slavery!
A slow burn Karma sutra
That slowly but surely took a toll on your spirit They shoot on sight at any silhouette susceptible to be the next Messiah
Wings broken, state of mind worsens, wrong deity
Nowadays, the Universal God is Money*

You don't have any? Ah! So sorry, but not really. When the hands of everyone else around you are so dirty
The best you can do is keep yours clean with the precious help of your integrity
Trying to stay focused
As they constantly find new ways to undermine us
Desperately in the need for the next Necessary Evil What do they do?
They create one on their own
Gurus of self-righteousness Wanting a unique thought streaming Heading toward the same direction Spiritual masturbation!
Mind's castration! Lies' lethal injection!
Giving you the right by them to be blessed
Now our freedom access is denied
For having lived with excess in that kingdom that is about to expire
The distorted time is about to digest all our ulcerous crimes
These superfluous placebos of spoiled existences
This is not living! It's barely surviving!
An emotions' washing!
A tremendous smoke screen
While people scream, scream, SCREAM!
The world seems always more colorful, full of room
And opportunities
Through the eyes of an army of scarecrows Like a torrential rain covering the beautiful sky with a stygian rainbow
While it's raining a myriad of Atomic mushrooms And that phosphorus is sprinkling cities
They're all pointing their infernal nuclear crossbows
And are willing to blow everything

Forgetting that under the same shelter we're all living
While death is smiling Living each new morning Like a delightful mourning
Contemplating the favorite hobby of mankind This endless infernal circle filled with genocides
Look, don't you notice the size of my dick? So, shut up and let me make you my bitch! More and more power
Makes them believe they have the biggest boner!
They're pointing the clock face As a foretaste
'You gonna be late for your life!'
They make us believe that each new day is the ends times
So that useless stuffs you can buy
Making you paranoid, glorifying the power of arms
While you're about to going... **VOLATILE**!
Be careful. You're maybe seeing right now a mere bunch of suckers
But it doesn't take much more for a bunch of suckers than:
Humiliation, lies, murders & Genocides! To eventually become **VOLATILE**!
So, don't be surprised
If you wake up one day surrounded by a bunch of suckers **VOLATILE**!
Cause you maybe see right now only Human merchandise
But it doesn't take much more for Human merchandise than:
Humiliation, lies, murders & Genocides! To eventually become **VOLATILE**!
So, don't you be surprised
If you wake up one day surrounded by Human merchandise **VOLATILE**!
Each new day is an opportunity to make things up Each new day is an opportunity to screw things up

Decade after decade spent on grilling brains or poisoning veins
Based on arbitrary accusations Wrong origin, color or religion Has always been the perfect reason
Using religions and turning simple minds Into time bombs
Using the flag to send simple minds
Transform peaceful lands into a devastated vision full of tombs Who's right? Who's wrong?
All I'm damn sure about is that only we will be responsible for our own extinction
While our ecosystem is choking Earthquakes as the very last electroshock To us he's sending
In response to our perpetual bad vibrations Warning us that it's still time to take action
Playing with frightened peoples mind Promising them promised lands or even a better after-life
And while buildings are blown up
And unnecessary armies fall like a sad rain of red snow
They try to make us swallow Their truth falsified
Smothered under rubble of underlying shameless lies
A web of fragmented painful memories Full of selfish feelings
They want to clothe your skin So, they can wash all their sins While you're suffocating
Frustration, Modernization, Deforestation, Oppression, Mystification
Too many moments of shame Instead of moments of grace
Having none concern for this shelter that is about to fail us
The same way we failed it Ignoring his warnings While we're admiring all these giant useless buildings
Sending us many signs Telling us that it's still time
But that it's in a very critical state And soon it will be too late

*Gun democratization, Deception, Arbitrary demonization
Makes you point out your frustration In the wrong direction
And leaves us with too many unanswered questions
And only one suggestion As a poor consolation...
Perpetual rape of the have-not's existence Makes us live our life under a perpetual creepy surgical ambiance
Trying to pigeonhole us all Into this godforsaken shithole
Pretending difference is a marginalization sign When all they see in us is another falling star Each of our heartbeat is a countdown
Whetting the infernal needles of their Doomsday Clock
Pointing us as the false note
I wish I could fly
So that I could get high
And not see this place for what it is
Upside down lands This huge soil
Full of disillusioned souls A morbid puddle
Full of individuals puzzled
Led by this colony of insignificant brainless ants Using their brainpower to build an army of nuclear power plants
Converting our pure original sanctum Into a huge asylum
While these morticians drink comfortably Their full-flavored coffee
Plaguing the Earth with too many coffins And turning lands into a huge cemetery
Always counting on an authority figure Leaving our Ozone Layer
With as many scars
As Universe has dead stars
Cause even the all world's ink Couldn't erase their lack of will
When facts corroborate The words*

Showing us how we failed To save our own world
Each of their appearing is preceded by an Imperial March
While they're trying to cover their ass
By covering their face with motionless wax mask Deadpan expression
Behind which they hide their inaction Disguising into a commonplace fact Something looking like a booby trap
Nuclear arsenals, climate change, carbon emissions and perpetual endless conflicts Serving only personal interests of a few unscrupulous fellowships
Nowadays, learn how to kill
Is that the kind of shit we want for our kids? Taking advantage of their fragile little mind Making them believe they're king Compassion? Love?
What the hell does that even mean?
Making them believe they aren't going to die If on the top of their building
They would try to fly
We're constantly so eager to see what tomorrow's going to look like
Without even giving today at least a shot Without imagining what the past might have looked like
Without all these pointless fights
Each one trying to prove he has the biggest dick Always the same competitive spirit
*Screwing with life with the same twisted mind Instead of becoming... **VOLATILE**!*
And now we are waiting... Waiting for a new perception Waiting for a new vision
A new revelation Without any disillusion
To solve once and for all this endless equation...

Outro: **Ruse de Sioux**
I'd like to be a bee-pollinator so that fruits and vegetables I can be pollinating
Be part of this magnificent cooperative self- organizing
I'd like to be a scorpion
To piss off some of these jerks full of selfish feelings
With my sting
And then, hide under the sand my bad actions
I'd like to be a butterfly
So that before the end of the day I may die
And not have to witness tomorrow's genocides
I'd like to drink tea
In the middle of the desert's immensity Far away from these CAUTION panels Just this peaceful vision of sand
Far away from these perpetual construction of panels
Just my tea and a share of watermelon I long... I long...
Now, I'm just standing before the sea Waiting for the next wave
Wondering if she will wash my sins away I long... I long...
I can't even remember when it started Am I capable to tell when it will end?
Probably when everything will be completely damned
Our past looks like a first draft
A prelude to a pointless last final blast When people are afraid of the backlash, all they're left with is a cop out
So, become **Volatile** before them
By becoming this unexpected alternative end...

<u>RAMIFICATIONS</u>

Intro: Wanderer
Sun, sun, sun My friend Don't be so shy
Share with me a bit of your shine

I imagine a giant heavenly battle
Soldiers falling from the sky like fallen angels The sky is crying his bravest stars
As a magnificent universal flag
Look, don't you see?
The sun's smiling his sunshine for us Burning our sins
Till it leaves nothing but a desert of dust
His sweet heat comforts our poor soul Printing with his shadow a carpet on the soil
I've always wondered
How many could there be of words? Millions... Billions? A world
An entire world full of words
From everywhere, People flock
To see if anywhere else there's an ounce of hope
Too many soldiers In this world
Not enough saviors...
The world isn't going to change Overnight
The Past stays the past
From which Present seems to follow the tracks
Little soldier please go home Give up this madness
Don't be a slave to this so-called moral
Patriotism should never be an excuse for genocides
Everything is neither black nor white
Not just good or just bad
Don't let some morons telling you where the limit is If yes or no you can cross the line
Sometimes it's easier to follow orders of some greedy blind guy
Who telling you to kill a stranger for the honor of the flag
Sometimes it's easier to believe in the best tagline
Of a death salesman

While we're getting more & more used to this daily background noise of shelling Drum sounds that became nothing but inspirations for a Requiem
The borders all around the world Made us perfect strangers
Stone hearts hating each other Supremacy of non-democracies Governed by a media blitz
Telling you who's your friend, who's your enemy What to think, what story must we swallow Making us mindless goats, killing in cold blood And all of that in the name of God or black gold The truth is never easy to tell
And sometimes we prefer not to think by ourselves Believing what others say
Everybody has his own reason To sink into unreason
Everyone has to face to his own demons
Let's be smarter than our predecessors Let's break these borders
Let's stop following orders
And as corny and naive as it may sound Let's fight with flowers Even though I quite know that it never stopped them before And that there will be many petals and bullets on the floor before the end of this age of terror
Let Time kill everyone
Instead of continuing this perpetual genocide As hobby to kill time

UNFORTUNATELY...

Peace's running out of time While War's ruling our time Unfortunately...
It seems that Earth, for peace, isn't the right place to be Into each heart grows a personal conflict While only one feeling subsists

Leaving none room for peace to exist
Unfortunately...
It seems than the human heart, for peace, isn't the right place to be
Unfortunately...
We've sold our mind
To an endless depression
To the contemplation of a decline
Watching inside our bubble Our own world's rubble
I've contemplated a myriad of colors Coming out from a single wide-open flower Witnessed the mystification
Of the bravest chameleon Mystifying his natural predator With the thousands colors
He borrowed to this magnificent flower The subjugating awakening of a volcano Spiting its wrath
In a splendid magma blast
I've admired the bravery of a whale
Facing her imminent death on this carpet of sand Drowning herself in slow agony
Lying upon this ocean of a billion suns
Until Blue became Black Until hope comes back
Hope will come from the dark Hope will come from the night
We don't need another religion We don't want another nation
We want our own awakening We want to be part of all things
We want the chameleonizing of our skin

4

Smoking his cigarette, Martial is still standing before the church. His eyes are fixated on the top of the church's steeple.
    The sky is cloudy and gloomy.

"I miss you little troublemaker... Troublemakers..." says Martial to himself, morosely.

Martial then stares lengthily at the entrance of the church... pondering... reminiscing...

5

DECEMBER 1967

The majority of the inhabitants of Rocky Tank Town are sitting in pews listening to Sunday mass given by the Reverend Tom Matterson, "...then a branch will emerge and a shoot will grow from its roots. The spirit of the lord will rest on Him, the spirit of wisdom and understanding, the spirit of counsel and strength, the spirit of knowledge and the fear of the lord."

Sitting in the front row is Neil Slatie wearing a black suit and a tie, while his cane is right next to him, propped up against the pew. Beside him is his wife, Stella Slatie, who is wearing a black dress, and finally Marcia and an eleven-year-old May Sissy. Both are dressed in the same long black dress with lace collars, while their hair is always tied in a low bun.

And as the Reverend Matterson is delivering mass, the church doors make a very slight squeak that no one seems to notice, except the lively and curious May Sissy who turns instinctively, but discreetly toward the doors. She sees Martial, then fourteen years old, and his mother Mindy enter. It is the first time she sees Martial. Martial wears a black suit and a black tie. Mindy is wearing a conservative skirt and a white top. She discreetly signals Martial to sit quietly on the empty pew to their right. Martial obeys and joins his mother on the bench. They're the only two people sitting on the bench. From an early age Martial's mother was very curious, which was quite unusual for a black woman. Mostly for someone who lived in a macho community where men feared that knowledge and wisdom might someday fall into the hands of women. She grew up in a farm in Texas until the age of fourteen and a half, then her uncle decided she was old enough to be a wife. Her uncle was the owner of a small shop selling chainsaws until he went belly up. One day in May 1952, he received a visit from a black customer who told him of his intention to marry. Mindy's uncle thought it was a sign of destiny and offered him a quite unexpected deal. He told him that he had a niece named Mindy aged thirteen and free. The deal was that, in exchange for marrying his niece, the client must acquire his chainsaws store. This was agreed upon by a manly handshake in order to honor a rather sordid, but common deal at that time, unbeknownst to the young and innocent girl somewhere in Texas. So, she left her native farm to go somewhere in Oregon, where she was married to Asa Furrows at the age of thirteen and a half years. He was twenty-seven years old. Nine months later, on September 16, 1953, she gave birth to her first and only child. Unfortunately, the purchase of the chainsaw store by Asa was never to be honored, because Mindy's uncle died two months later of his addiction to the bottle, an addiction he passed on to his son, in addition to his store. As for Asa, he was called to South Vietnam in 1956 where for a brief moment he met a man, Stephen Misniwill, as they took a piss side by side. The two men exchanged one of the most moving conversations: *'Damn country!'* To which Stephen retorted *'Damn right!'* War sometimes had this strange power to make people forget differences about their origins. So a black man and a white man could easily exchange a few words quietly like childhood friends while pissing against a palm tree as bombs exploded all around them. This is something you couldn't even imagine back in the States at that time. But hey, this is a story as old as the world itself and built on a great philosophy: *The enemy of my enemy is my friend*. Or more accurately: *As long as they slaughter Viet Cong, these niggers are our equals... until the war is over anyway.*

Mindy became a widow at the age of seventeen years and raised her son alone the best she could, which at that time was not easy for a seventeen-year-old black woman with a three-year-old child. However, having gone to school until the age of twelve and a half, she could read and write and even knew some basic Latin. She rolled up her sleeves and found a job at the post office in Oregon. She worked Monday through Friday from seven a.m. to three p.m. One day as she was sorting the mail, she came across an envelope that said 'ROCKY TANK TOWN, NIOBRARA, WYOMING'. So, the day she realized she had put enough money aside after ten years of hard work, she thought it was time to take a fresh start somewhere else, somewhere ideal if possible. What place could be more ideal than Wyoming? A precursor state, the first to grant voting rights to women and elect a woman as governor in 1925. More importantly, she had heard Rocky Tank Town was a very small town, isolated from everything, sometimes even forgotten by the government, with no census, and since this damn Vietnam War kept producing more deaths than victories, she secretly hoped that once settled there she would have a chance to see her only son not be called to duty to end up as her husband did. So, in December 1967, Mindy and Martial arrived in Rocky Tank Town, where Mindy raised Martial as best she could, until his departure in 1970. Despite her rigor, she always had a sharp sense of humor and always liked to think The Lord had a sense of humor too and could tolerate some small jabs against him. Belief in a religion was a strictly personal business. Her whole life was guided by a philosophy of tolerance and openness.

While the voice of the Reverend Matterson still reaches May Sissy's ears, she seems more interested in Martial and Mindy sitting on the empty pew at the back of the church. Until of course her mother notices her daughter's distraction and scolds her in a hushed voice:

"May Sissy?"

May Sissy turns her head toward her mother. She almost forgot she is in a church. Marcia beckons her to look straight ahead and nowhere else while the Reverend continues his mass:

"He shall fear the Lord.

"He shall not judge by the appearance.

"He will not pronounce on hearsay. But He will judge the poor with equity, and pronounce with equity on the meek of the earth.

"He shall smite the earth his speech as a rod, and the breath of his lips.

"He shall slay the wicked. Justice shall be the girdle of his loins, and faithfulness the girdle of his reins.

"The wolf shall dwell with the lamb, and the leopard shall lie down with the goat, the calf and the young lion and livestock be fattened, will be together, and a small child shall lead them. The cow and the bear shall share the same pasture; their young shall lie down together; and the lion, like the ox shall eat straw. The sucking child shall play on the hole of the asp, and the weaned child shall put his hand in the cave basilisk. It will neither harm nor destroy on my entire holy mountain, for the earth is full of the knowledge of the Lord, as the bottom of the sea which waters cover it. In that day, the offspring of Isaiah shall stand as a banner for the people; the nations will rally to him, and the glory will be his dwelling. At that time, the Lord extends his hand a second time, to redeem the remnant of his people…"

6

<u>IN PAIN, IN VAIN</u>
I used to be the kid who was taking the beating. I used to be the kid always avoiding the fight. I'm the man who, from reality, took a huge smack
I used to be the kid who was taking the beating. Now I'm the man who finally got into a fight
Too bad
We're never shielded from our biggest enemy, Because, like in my childhood
By reality
I've been screwed
God is not there He doesn't care
Too busy playing dead Leaving an endless void That we can't avoid
What is the point of contemplating the sky When you know it's full of corrupt stars? What's the point of waiting for God's sign? God is hypocritical
Hiding behind the so-called 'Free will' The fact that our blind love for him Isn't reciprocal.

7

Martial is now looking toward Raven's Feathers while

reminiscing a nice memory of the past. His gaze is now suddenly filled with regret and sadness. More than ever, he misses the precious company of the young, fearless and joyful May Sissy. Martial suddenly feels overwhelmed by this strange feeling, a feeling belonging to a memory stranger to him. A memory pre-dating his own earthly existence. That's what it feels like anyway. Martial realizes that the more he witnesses pure beauty, the more his bitterness feeds on his melancholia. He comes to the painful realization that a nice memory can be corrupted either by suddenly coming to the realization that time has passed, and you'll never be able to duplicate this perfect and idealized context, or by... a tragic event.

And as he stares at the magnificent map above him, Martial loses himself inside the maze of his mind, with no guarantee of coming back.

8

SEPTEMBER 17, 1968
May Sissy and Martial are standing just before the secondary entrance at Raven's Feather, contemplating this splendid spectacle offered to them. The beautiful, spellbinding cornflower blue sky with a timid nuance of reddish-purple. The whole view forming a mesmeric work of art. A pure panoramic vastness of magnificence tinged with a hint of melancholy.

The heavens offer May Sissy and Martial their perfect visual requiem-like Ode.

"What a hypnotizing spectacle!" May Sissy says, admiring the painting above her.

"Yeah, but there's something a bit sad about it," says Martial, also admiring the fresco above him.

"Perfection always inspires a bit of melancholy," answers May Sissy while looking up at the sky in bewilderment.

"Yeah. I wonder why," ponders Martial.

The perfection May Sissy contemplates is reflecting in the two tiny galaxies that are her eyes as she says,

"I think our hearts cannot bear so much beauty. And somehow it becomes this melancholy we feel. Well, that's what I think anyway."

9

Smoking his cigarette, Martial is still standing outside the church. And as he stares lengthily at the entrance of the church Martial remembers a phrase his mother used to say to him: *'It is not because we all aspire to go to heaven that we must allow our life to be a living hell!'*

Some people's story arc can be ripped from them, unfairly denied. Some people's family tree can be brutally uprooted, never to grow back, leaving instead a gap. A bottomless well filled with repressed memories. Leaving you staring at this heavenly map, desperately searching for a life guide.

Throwing his cigarette butt on the ground, Martial finally decides to enter the church…

POETIC EPILOGUE

ELEPHANT GRAVEYARD

'If the road to hell is paved with good intentions, then what about paradise?'
MAY SISSY MISNIWILL -

WINDOW OF TIME
Is it my fault if while you admire it all All I manage to see is a black hole? If, to you, Time is a whole?
It's not for want of trying But,
Strength is a bygone feeling Of my pain it is feeding
And I know now I'll never see the sky as Blue As you do
When endless shades of shame Is all you're able to feel When everything is only pain Self-destruction is the result of a lifetime of autosuggestions?
When you're unable to stop focusing on the brevity of your life
When you're unable to stop living your life as a half empty glass
The light at the end of the tunnel
Has always been my cloak of illusions Idealizing my life's conclusion
Life is just a succession of seasons Life is all about choosing the weather that best suits your character
And when the time comes Letting go of your ego
Sometimes inaction seems the best reaction
Life... Love... passion... Giving us a reason to embrace our fate

But sometimes it feels like too much is at stake
It's too late
The world isn't able to satisfy my needs Death... Suicide...
Maybe from the very beginning I've chosen the wrong side
Time is playing my song
Letting me know it's my cue to leave
Sometimes inaction seems the best action
I've got my ticket For the final step
I don't wish to put my life on hold
But nor do I wish to see myself getting old
And I know now I'll never see the sky as Blue As you do
A single brief moment sometimes is enough to mourn someone
Sometimes
A lifetime isn't enough to fully get to know somebody
Sometimes
Life feels like a brief instant A short window of time
A future disguised into Present
Time rusts all things
And makes you forget everything
Like a venom poisoning your mind and skin Making of them souvenirs dust
Leaving only an empty skull
Making your skin lose the habit of touch
To eventually leave a skin as scaly as the rust
I've once cherished the dream
Of one day be able to take the leap Stop to do the splits
Wipe this goddamn perpetual cold sweat
Walking on this fine thread Like a tight-rope walker
Living my life as a game of poker
Sometimes I feel like if I had never stop to play at the jump-rope Jumping perpetually from one side to the other

Always about to drop when I see that both sides offer no hope
I've had once cherished the hope But now it's gone up in smoke
Needles of Time
Are poisoning our veins
Making us addicted to our watch While we're trying to go back in time
By trying to corrupt the clock in our mind
My blood vessels are just like a tunnel railway But it's too late anyway!
I had a train to catch only once and I let it get away Missing the window
But leaving me one last still open to jump Oh! too kind!
A one-way ticket out of this dump That has become my mind
Having been left to my own fate
Showing me it hasn't the intention to save me a piece of cake I decided to skip this complete farce
And pass to the final act And by sleight of hand (Poof!)
I simply skip to the end! Cause I don't fit the character
So, I pass, offering you as well my best cliffhanger!

THE BUTTERFLY'S PURPOSE
Each new dawn gives birth to a stillborn day
The idea to communicate each other crosses our mind But once again we go on our separate way
Intending to concretize this fantasy to some other time
I looked at the sun Sun looked at me
And we aged together...
Or perhaps, was it only me (?)
I close my eyes
On this peaceful heaven But does it mean
At the next eventide We will be even?

Time seems to take pleasure
To, upon me, put more and more pressure
While I am looking for a voice to speak on behalf of my anger
I looked at the moon Moon looked at me And we aged together...
Or perhaps, it was only me?
Perhaps tomorrow will be my chance of redemption A perfect Transition
Delaying the inevitable Time mystification
I'm willing to embrace my inevitable downfall Lose myself into the fragmented web of the nightfall Willing to share pieces of my soul
I looked at today Today looked at me And we aged together...
Or perhaps, was it only me?
Time confronts all dreams
To the cruel reality that the time flies Leaving our mind full of fragmented pieces of moments
But I know I can still rely on the night to prove the time is wrong
Today is still young
Tonight, I will be dreaming of a bridge called: Between
Hoping to end this Monotony
Wishing that tomorrow, of today Will not be the twin
I looked at yesterday Yesterday looked at me And we aged together...
Or perhaps, was it only me?
I will look at tomorrow Tomorrow will look at me Yet... tomorrow
Will I still be?

ELEPHANT GRAVEYARD
I was searching for the Eldorado Only to find the last resting place of my brothers
Eldorado is dead witnessing a slaughter
I was searching for the Eldorado Only to find the last resting place of my brothers
Eldorado is dead
Wiped off the map by a Human Sirocco
I can hear almost everything... Can you?
I can feel almost everything... You too?
(It's so calm!)
Slaves of our own memories Meanders we try to forget
But painfully force us to remember It's hard to comfort a broken heart
Not having one, would maybe be easier
All I wanted was to be spared You used to be my outlet
As I was yours
(It's so calm!) Since you left
While icy wind of a long winter is about to blast (It's so calm!)
Right now I feel like all around me is about to die
Like thousands pieces of glass falling right from the sky (It's so calm!)
All I wanted was to be spared
It's hard to comfort a broken heart Not having one, would maybe be easier You used to be my outlet
As I was yours (It's so calm!) Since you left
Leaving me alone with my fears Drowning myself in my own tears
While on my shoulders the reality became too hard to bear
Leaving me alone in this world of despair
(It's so calm!)

Without your presence Everything has its limits
And now all that is left to me is your absence And my mind's decadence
All I wanted was to be spared You used to be my outlet
As I was yours (It's so calm!) Since you left
My gaze is searching for my long gone outlet
Lost into this receptacle full of unfamiliar silhouettes
Dear friend,
I don't know what you're up to I wish you the best
Hoping you're not going through Hell Like I do
I wanted to live Hell set me on fire I've nothing to fear I've already burned
Ripped apart has been my soul
Leaving me with nothing but this taste of not feeling whole
A gaping wound
In the center of which for too long you stood
I've been running after your shadow For far too long
Only to realize that I became A shadow of myself
Maybe it's now time to stop being a long gone ghost's widow
The bleakness of my mind walls is more and more a too-hard to bear hangover Perhaps it's now time to admit you've been this Blindside-picture
I finally killed the Debbie downer in me This genie in the bottle I set free
You'll never know how much I loved you I suppose it is for the best
I just needed to get that out of my chest
Look at me now!
Soulless as a clone, devoid of any fate This body, my soul doesn't fit
I think I'm losing it

I start hearing the voices of my dormant madness Realizing that it could rip a great benefit out of my loneliness
Ephemeral love finding inside this ink river its last resting place
(It's so calm!)
I'm now facing this army of pines Like thousands of great vassals Faithful, full of bravery
But yet, making me feel like surrounded by an atmosphere filled with tragedy
What is this weight on my shoulders? Why am I feeling this invisible collier? Chaining up my mind to this last memory of you
The sound of your shackles spoke to me
I know now what you must've gone through.